ɔer Bag Christmas

ok is a work of fiction. All characters are fictional and any resem-
to persons living or dead is purely coincidental.

Distributed by:

GRANITE
PUBLISHING & DISTRIBUTION L.L.C.

Granite Publishing and Distribution, LLC
868 North 1430 West
Orem, Utah 84057
(801) 229-9023 • Toll Free (800) 574-5779
Fax (801) 229-1924

Cover Design by Tammie Ingram
Page Layout and Design by Myrna Varga

ISBN-13: 978-1-56684-642-4
ISBN-10: 1-56684-642-0
Library of Congress Control Number: 2006962015

3 5 7 9 10 8 6 4 2

Manufactured in the United States of America

Printed by FC Printing, Salt Lake City, UT

2008

KEEP writing!

THE

Paper B

Chr

by

KEVIN ALAN MI

THE

Paper Bag Christmas

To my wife Rebecca, without whom
I'd have very little.
And also to my father and mother—thanks
for not naming me Molar.

Prologue

"Happy, happy Christmas, that can win us back to the delusions of our childhood days, recall to the old man the pleasures of his youth, and transport the traveler back to his own fireside and quiet home!"

❁ Charles Dickens ❁

Two words: Merry Christmas or perhaps Happy Christmas if such fits your geographic predilection. Two words so full of promise, but all too often relegated to commonplace by the jingling bells of wanting that accompany the season. Yet for those most fortunate few who stumble across its underlying significance, Merry Christmas becomes a treasure trove of good will—a miraculous gift, waiting just beyond the oft hollow words to be opened and enjoyed by all who comprehend it.

To fully understand the inherent goodness of the occasion, one must first experience a *real* Christmas. When that occurs, it becomes far more than just another holiday or a prolonged shopping spree. Christmas becomes a part of you: an ideal and a desire for others instead of oneself. It becomes, in short, a paper bag.

A paper bag? Yes, precisely. But not just any paper bag, mind you. It becomes a weathered, wrinkled, dirty paper bag, the kind you'd just as soon throw out with yesterday's trash if you didn't know its history. A paper bag so soiled and lowly that it could only be used for one final purpose: as a lasting and irreplaceable reminder of why we celebrate at all.

Sadly, only a lucky few will ever encounter the likes of a *real* Christmas and the lasting joy it brings. Fewer still are lucky enough to know firsthand about the paper bag.

I am one of the lucky ones.

The day after Thanksgiving, 1980, marked the beginning of my first *real* Christmas. As a nine-year-old boy I had certainly celebrated the revered holiday plenty of times before, but that particular Christmas was the first one that really mattered. It was the type of experience that makes you wish Christmas was celebrated all year long, the kind that makes people forget about life's imperfections and focus instead on its greatest treasures. For me it was a defining moment, one that has shaped and molded the very fabric of my soul.

I'm Molar Alan, and this is my story. It is as real to me as the Santa of my youth, and I share it with an enduring hope that you will carry its message beyond the realm of reindeer, elves, or toys, and embed it deep in your heart where the distractions and disappointments of life can't enter, where the worldly can look but not touch, and where the rich in spirit can come and go at will.

As with many Christmas stories, mine began on Santa's lap. But this was no ordinary Santa, and he had anything but an ordinary lap.

CHAPTER

One

"I stopped believing in Santa Claus when I was six. Mother took me to see him in a department store and he asked for my autograph."

❁ Shirley Temple ❁

With Thanksgiving dinner less than 12 hours gone by, the house still smelled of pumpkin pie and green bean casserole. Mello sounds of Bing Crosby drifting in from the record player in the parlor blended curiously with cheers of football fans roaring from the television in the living room. Food, Bing, and football: the Christmas season had officially begun, in all of its holiday glory.

My brother and I were knee deep in leftover turkey sandwiches when my parents entered the kitchen. "Let's go guys," said my father excitedly as he pulled on his rain slicker and joined us at the counter. "Its time to go see the big man!"

"Grandpa?" I asked as I wiped a smudge of mayonnaise from my cheek.

"No, not that big man. The other one. The big man in the big red suit!"

"Oh no," I mumbled.

"Oh yes! We're going to see Santa Claus!" He let the name

roll slowly off his tongue for dramatic effect.

Our lack of excitement didn't seem to bother him.

"Do we have to?" asked my brother Aaron. "I mean, aren't we too old for that?"

Aaron was two years older than me and had long since figured out that the Santa Claus at the mall wasn't the *real* Santa Claus.

"Besides," Aaron continued, "if there was a Santa Claus, I'm sure he wouldn't spend his Thanksgiving vacation at a mall in Oregon where it is always raining. He'd be down in Florida or somewhere nice. So why should we even bother?"

"I disagree," countered my mother as she strode across the room. "He would be . . . I mean he *is* in Oregon enjoying this rain. In fact, he has to come here over Thanksgiving so he can pick up his reindeer! Get it? *Rain* deer."

We got it but didn't give her the satisfaction of a laugh.

"That's right boys," piped dad. "Besides, its tradition to tell Santa what you want for Christmas. And if you break tradition, you might not get what you want this year. Now go put on your coats. We want to beat the holiday rush."

❋ ❋ ❋

By the time we arrived at the mall all thoughts of beating the holiday rush were replaced by a desperate hope that we could simply find a parking spot. Inside was no better. People swarmed around from store to store laden with their bags and boxes and precious things.

The line to see Santa stretched nearly three hundred feet, from a small wooden cabin in the middle of the mall right on past a store that sold nothing but socks. A large hand-painted sign across the cabin doorway read "The Santa Shack: A Little Taste of The North Pole." Apparently the North Pole tastes like candy canes because elves in sparkling green robes and dark purple tights paraded around the tiny structure handing out the white and red striped candy to every man, woman, and child that entered.

Another elf stood alone near the end of the line. He was handing out red pieces of paper and pencils to each of the children as they approached the growing queue.

"What's this for?" I asked when he handed me a paper.

"Its for you's to make a list to give to Santi Claus, little boy." The man spoke through a broken smile as he lowered himself down to look me straight in the eyes.

"You talk funny," I said. Although I was nine I had not yet figured out how to keep my brutally honest thoughts to myself.

"That right?" He laughed. "Well you's should know that back in da Bronx you'd sound funny, too."

"Sorry mister," I offered. I was glad he didn't take it personally.

"So how come we have to write our list down? Can't we just tell him when we get up there?"

"We figure since you's gonna be here in line a while, you might as well make good use of da time, ya know? That way you don't have to think of nothin' to say to da big man when it's your turn, 'cuz it'll already be on your list. Just hand him your paper and move along. Understand?"

I nodded affirmatively.

"Good." He ruffled my hair with his hand as he stood up. "Merry friggin Christmas," he added.

I looked at the paper and read the title at the top of the page: *All I Want For Christmas Is. . .* Other than those few words, the paper was full of blank lines, three columns wide on both the front and back. Perhaps enough to write down every toy and gadget I'd ever seen in my entire life.

My parents asked the man how long the wait was.

"Well," he said as his eyes darted back and forth between the crowded line and his wrist watch. "I ain't exactly timing it or nothin' 'cuz of my other important 'sponsibilities." He held up the stack of paper and pencils. "But I'd say about an hour, maybe more. Course, you's all need to keep in mind that at twelve o'clock sharp, jolly ole' Saint Nick up there's gonna take a break for two hours. If you ain't seen him by then it's just your bad luck."

Mom and Dad decided they would leave us in line by ourselves while they did some shopping for 'some very important people' who remained nameless. Aaron was left in charge even though I felt more than competent in my ability to take care of myself at the mall. So there we were, two brothers stranded at the end of what seemed like an endless line, waiting for our chance to hand over our Christmas lists to some stranger dressed up as Santa Claus.

With nothing else to do we began filling in the blanks on our papers. At first the list was easy to write as my desires poured onto the page like Oregon rain on a winter night. But after a short while the task proved to be a more difficult than either of us would have thought. The top item on my list was an Air Jammer Road Rammer, a sleek yellow and black toy car that ran solely on the power of hand-pumped air. It was undoubtedly the hottest toy of the year based on the frequency of its commercials during Saturday morning cartoons. Next I wrote a pogo stick, a glow-in-the-dark yo-yo, some stickers, and a rubber-band gun.

After that I had to think a little harder. I reasoned that Santa would likely start at the top of my list and then work his way down, so I began ordering my desires based on how much joy I anticipated each item would bring me during the upcoming year. The list continued but at a much slower pace: a dog, a new baseball glove, a brine shrimp chemistry set, a. . . .

"Aaron, how do you spell trampoline?" I asked.

"Just like it sounds, dumbo. T-r-a-m-p-o-l-l-e-e-n." I could tell he liked that idea, too because he wrote the word on his list while he spelled it out.

Within a few minutes the expanse of my youthful mind became so empty that I had to seek ideas in the world around me in order to keep the list growing. I saw one boy with a ring-pop lollipop on his finger. Bingo! Ring-pop was added to my list. Another boy had a neat hat, a girl was bouncing a rubber ball, and a man walked by carrying a new set of roller skates for some lucky child. Each item was quickly jotted down.

Then out of the corner of my eye, I saw the jackpot, the mother load of Christmas goodies: toy store! It had more items in the window than I could count. Action figures, stuffed animals, puzzles, games, cards, cars, slinkies, and silly putty were all there. Everything I could ever want all packaged nicely under one roof, and each item made it to my list. Before long my paper was filled with a splendid array of childhood accessories, sufficient to bring even the most spoiled of children countless hours of delight.

Once we were close enough to Santa's Shack, we saw that the kids were doing just as the Bronx-elf had instructed. One by one they went in and handed their list to Santa. He looked it over briefly, gave them each a few parting words and a healthy 'Ho, Ho, Ho', and then they were done.

For some reason no one was allowed to sit on Santa's lap. A few parents grumbled that his ample waistline was off-limits, but most were just glad to get through the ordeal and be done with it for another year.

As we neared the entrance I began to get anxious. My parents had not yet returned, and it was almost twelve o'clock. In just a few minutes Santa was going to take a break from his merrymaking, and if we weren't through the line by then we wouldn't be able to hand him our list for at least another two hours.

When we finally reached the doorway of the Santa Shack we found ourselves standing next to a tall blonde elf wearing red lipstick, purple high heels, black fishnet stockings, which matched her black leather skirt, and a green v-neck jumper to top it all off.

"Where do they find these people?" I snickered under my breath to my brother, who was staring at the woman in disbelief.

"Shhhh!" he hissed accusingly. "I think she's a famous actress from a soap opera or something."

"No way. Why would a famous person be in charge of the line to see Santa Claus?"

"Well," he thought. "Maybe it's charity work."

I checked her out thoroughly once more. "Maybe."

"Um excuse me, mam," said Aaron breathlessly to the woman as he slicked back his hair. "The elf at the back of the line is from New York. Are you by any chance from California? Hollywood perhaps?"

A rush of excitement coursed through us as the blonde elf turned to look, first at my brother, then at me. I smiled wide as our eyes met, but the thrill of the moment was over before it even began. She gave us both an unsavory stare, curling her upper lip and rolling her eyes just enough to show her disdain. Then without so much as a single word, she returned to what she had been doing before our verbal intrusion, which was noisily chewing gum while watching the seconds tick away on a nearby clock.

Inside the cabin, the little girl who was ahead of us in line had just finished her brief interlude with Santa when the tall blonde finally found something to say. "Lunch Time!" she shouted. "That's it kids! Come back in two hours!"

She smirked in our general direction as she grabbed a chain and strung it across the doorway, blocking our entrance to Santa's inner sanctum. Then she turned and strutted silently away.

CHAPTER

Two

"When we were children we were grateful to those who filled our stockings at Christmas time. Why are we not grateful to God for filling our stockings with legs?"

❁ Gilbert K. Chesterton ❁

"It's not fair," I whined. "All that waiting, only to be turned away at the last possible moment!"

"No kidding," shrugged Aaron. "You know, I didn't really want to come this morning, but as long as we stood in that stupid line we should at least get to see Santa, right?"

With the line dissipating behind us, Aaron and I agreed that our long morning wait had earned us a closer look into the cabin so we skirted around the chain and pressed our faces up to one of the windows. To our surprise, Santa was staring calmly back at us from his elaborate, wintry throne.

He had soft, searching eyes. His face was covered with a fake but believable beard, and his large belly bounced slightly when he shifted his weight. Thick legs filled out his oversized red pants, which were stuffed carefully into shiny leather boots that rested squarely in front of him on the floor.

I knew he wasn't the *real* Santa, but I thought if there were a real Santa in the world he would probably look something like this.

We stood gaping at each other for what felt like minutes. Santa seemed to be waiting for something. When the crowds of children behind us had completely scattered, the man in the big red costume made the slightest of movements with his eyes.

"Does he want us to come in?" I whispered.

"Dunno," said Aaron.

Santa added a brisk head tilt to go along with his eye movements, but we still weren't sure if he was motioning to us or just fidgeting with his costume. When we didn't respond to his rolling eyes and head shaking, he made it more obvious.

"Would you two fine young men like to come in and show me your lists?" he asked. He spoke with a heavy Scottish accent that was warm and inviting.

"But the lady with the skirt said you're closed," I replied.

"Well, yes she did, lad. But she's only an elf after all. As the chief ambassador of Christmas, I think I can make a small exception for the Alan boys. You're Aaron, right?" he said, looking at my brother. "And you must be Molar."

"How do you know our names, mister?" asked Aaron.

"How else my boy? I'm Santa Claus! Ho! Ho! Ho!" He was grinning from ear to ear as he spoke. "Now go ahead; come on in for a wee minute. I think it's time you showed me what you want for Christmas."

"Sorry, whoever you are," said Aaron cautiously. "We'd love to come in, but I don't think our parents would want us in there alone. You know how it is."

As if on cue we heard a familiar call from nearby. Looking back behind us we saw Mom and Dad standing beside the fence that surrounded Santa's compound.

"It's okay guys. Go on in!" shouted Dad happily. He and Mother were both smiling and waving. "We'll wait right here until you're done."

As a general rule, Dad hated malls. He only came when he had to so he was probably overjoyed that we had been offered a way around the two hour break. With their permission we hustled back around to the front door and made our way up to stand before Santa's great chair.

"Well now. Molar, let's start with you since you're the youngest. By the way, do you prefer to be called Molar or Mo?"

"Either is fine, I suppose, but my friends call me Mo." I'd answered that question at least a thousand times over the years. I learned very early in life that Molar is not a very common name. Most people wanted to know how my parents came up with it, but not the guy in the Santa suit. He already knew.

"Then Mo it is," he said. "Now let me see if I remember correctly. Your father is a dentist, and he was smack dab in the middle of taking his dental boards when you were born."

"That's right!" I exclaimed.

"And so he named you Molar in honor of his favorite tooth. Correct?"

"Yep! How did you know that?" I was truly amazed.

A wry grin formed in the corner of his eyes then spread across his entire face. "Like I said before, I'm Santa Claus! Now then, how about showing me that list of yours?"

I started to hand him my list, but my eyes caught sight of Santa's massive legs, and I pulled the paper back quickly.

"Um, Mr. Claus," I said slowly. "My dad brought us here today because it's tradition. But it's also kind of a tradition to sit on Santa's lap. I don't really care one way or the other, but why don't you let any of the kids sit on you? That's what all of the other Santa Clauses do."

The smile faded slightly from his face as he considered my question. He seemed to be mulling over how best to respond, perhaps even debating whether he should answer the question at all.

"Well boys, I suppose you're old enough to hear the truth. The fact is that old Saint Nicholas doesn't have any legs. Not real ones anyway. I *would* let the children sit on my lap, but I think it would scare them too much."

"What do you mean you don't have any legs?" said Aaron. "I can see them right there."

"Of course you can. But those are, well, they are magical legs. You can see them even though they don't exist in reality. You care to try them out? C'mon, both of you jump up here on my lap and find out for yourselves. I'll not have you thinking that Santa's a liar."

Aaron and I were understandably confused. Why was a guy dressed up as Santa talking nonsense about magical legs? We looked at each other for a moment and then peeked out the window to make sure Mom and Dad were still keeping a watchful eye. Without a valid reason not to, we took him up on his offer, each of us leaping at the same time onto one of the giant legs which hung over the corner of his big chair. But as soon as we made contact, *Swoosh,* a loud burst of air swept out from beneath us as Santa's legs went as flat as pancakes.

"Ahhh!!" I screamed. I'm sure Aaron and I shouted in unison, but I could only hear myself through the thunderous waves of panic that swept through my body. I scrambled off the flattened lap as fast as I could. Aaron was already two steps ahead of me.

"Ho! Ho! Ho!!" roared Santa as he burst into a side-splitting laughter. For a few confused moments I wondered if I was part of some strange Christmas nightmare, which undoubtedly would end poorly for my brother and me.

Once I had collected myself, I looked again at the man laughing himself to tears. His paper-thin pants remained limp in front of him, still tucked into the shiny black boots. His stomach seemed to have thinned considerably as well. "I'm sorry boys, but that was absolutely hilarious! Without a doubt the funniest thing I've ever seen. But I didn't mean to frighten you."

"What happened to your legs?" I asked frantically. "They were right there!"

"Now take it easy, lad. I warned you; I don't have any legs—just two numb stumps where legs should be. What you saw before was a couple of air bags stuffed inside my trousers. It takes some doing to inflate them, but it certainly makes the kids feel better to see a Santa with legs and a fat belly. And it saves me a lot of explaining."

Glancing once more out the cabin window I saw that Mom and Dad were also laughing themselves sick. *Yeah, real funny*, I thought. *I'll probably be scarred for life, and everyone is laughing about it.*

"Are we on Candid Camera or something?" asked Aaron

sheepishly as he scanned the doors and ceiling for hidden camera equipment.

"No. I'm afraid not although that would have been a splendid idea! I suppose that little gag just put me forever on the naughty list. Still, in all fairness to me, it was your father who put me up to it."

"But what happened to your legs?" I repeated again.

"Well," he said as he lightly stroked his thick, white beard. "I have a secret to share, one which will likely not surprise either of you. Although I may look like Santa Claus, I am, in fact, just a regular old Joe. I'm a friend of your parents—known them for years I have. They came by earlier and told me you weren't too excited to come see Santa today, so they wanted me to have a little fun with you. As for the legs, well, those have been missing for more than half my life. I've still got some stubs down there." He rapped lightly on one of the two bumps below his belt line. "But the rest of my legs I lost in World War II. That, however, is another matter altogether and not something for you to worry about." He paused for a moment, allowing us time to take in everything he'd just said. "Now then, how about those lists? Mo, would you still like to show me what you want for Christmas?"

I was still reeling from the shock of having deflated Santa, but without another word I handed the man my red paper. I was, in fact, pleased to be able to share with him my grand accomplishment, even if he was wasn't the real Santa Claus. It had not been easy to do, but every single line on the page was filled in, and I figured he would appreciate my magnum opus.

Santa took the paper and flipped it over several times. "Oh dear," he said with a hint of sadness in his voice. The twinkle in his eyes dimmed noticeably. "Oh dear, indeed. This will never do."

At first I wasn't entirely sure I'd heard him correctly. Was this legless, Scottish, Santa-impersonator critiquing my Christmas list? The one that I'd spent so much time on? How on earth could he find fault with such a comprehensive inventory of, well, everything a child could ever want?

"Aaron, is your list this big, too?" Santa's expression looked quite somber. Aaron nodded his head while tucking his red paper behind his back. Santa cleared his throat before speaking again. "It pains me to say this lads, but you will not be getting all of that stuff for Christmas." He paused again, choosing his words carefully. "The things on your list are nice, I suppose. And yet, they miss the mark entirely when it comes to true Christmas joy. Boys, would you like to get something for Christmas better than everything you've written down?"

I could hardly imagine what could be better than all of that stuff. I*t must be something HUGE*, I thought. The raw excitement of receiving such a gift coursed through me as I nodded eagerly.

"Good. Since you've already shown me your list of everything you've ever wanted for Christmas, let's call this gift everything you've *never* wanted for Christmas. How does that sound?"

"Okay," I said. "But if we've never wanted it, how do you know we'll like it?"

"Oh you'll like it well enough. I promise. But there's a catch. If you want this gift, I'll need a little help from you—sort of like working to pay for it." Santa reached in his coat pocket and pulled out a slip of paper, then scribbled down some words. "Have your parents bring you to this address on Monday night at six o'clock sharp. I'll be there waiting for you. You'll be dressing up as elves. I'll bring the costumes. Okay?"

"Sure," responded Aaron. "If you say so."

"Then it's settled. I'll see you on Monday. Now I really must start my break, and I'll have to get my legs and belly re-inflated. Would one of you mind opening that closet and fetching me my magic sleigh?"

We both hustled over to find a wheelchair inside the closet. It was decked out with holly, mistletoe, ribbons and bows, and a small battery that powered a string of red and green flashing Christmas lights. Magic indeed! We pushed it over to the man, and he climbed aboard, steadying himself with his arms as he descended from Santa's throne. As he wheeled around to the doorway, he let out a loud departing farewell: "Ho, Ho Ho!! Merrr-rry Christmas!" And then he was gone.

CHAPTER

Three

"God is the God of men . . . and of elves."

❁ J. R. R. Tolkien ❁

By the time Monday night rolled around, I was perfectly desperate to go help Santa out as an elf. I had told all my friends at school about the strange encounter with Santa Claus and his deflating legs, but they didn't believe one word of it. I can't say I blame them for their skepticism, but I was slightly disappointed at the teasing it invoked. Looking back, I probably should have exaggerated less about my upcoming 'secret mission as an international elf spy.'

At the appointed time, Dad dropped us off at the address listed on the paper we'd been given (incidentally, he knew where we were going without bothering to look at the address). It was a Children's Hospital in downtown Portland. True to his word, the man we had met in Santa's cabin at the mall was waiting for us when we arrived. He no longer donned the red suit, but his 'sleigh' was still blinking red and green.

"Hello. How are you lads on this fine evening? Ready to help me out I hope." He looked very different without the hat and beard, but his eyes still twinkled with great depths of kindness.

"Boys," said Dad. "I'd like to formally introduce you to Dr. Ringle. When he's not moonlighting as Santa Claus, he works as a pediatric oncologist here at the hospital. Please be on your best behavior while you're helping him, okay? I'll pick you up in a few hours."

The hospital was decorated to the nines with wreaths and wrapping everywhere I gazed. A large glowing Christmas tree stood towering in the main lobby, adorned with popcorn strings, candy canes, and white crocheted doilies that dangled like falling snowflakes.

Dr. Ringle led us to a locker room where two elf costumes were waiting beside empty lockers. They looked very similar to those worn by the elves at the mall, only our tights were as yellow as the sun and plastered with red and green polka dots. *This,* I thought, *is Christmas gone awry.* We were also given special elfin booties that curled up at the toes which held several tiny bells that jingled incessantly with every step. To top it all off they required us to wear surgical masks and gloves so as not to spread any of our potentially harmful germs to the sick children, whose immune systems were already weak. It was a reasonable request given our surroundings, but it made for some awfully funny looking elves.

Dr. Ringle changed into his Santa costume too, only without his inflatable legs. Once we were all ready he led us up to the 5th floor of the hospital. On our way to the elevator, children and adults alike stopped whatever they were doing and stared unabashed as we passed by. A grand trio we made: Santa Claus with no legs in a blinking wheelchair being trailed by two glowing elves prepped for surgery.

The 5th floor was much quieter than the hospital's main level, but there was nevertheless a lot happening all around. Young children scampered from room to room making sure everyone knew that Santa and his helpers had finally arrived; nurses and parents busied themselves hanging holiday knick-knacks wherever space allowed. Outside each patient's room hung a fine hand-knit stocking, while the inside of every room was littered with decorations galore. Each boy and girl had their very own tiny Christmas tree centered on their windowsill between red and white poinsettias. Cards and other decorations hung from the ceilings, and the bed frames were adorned with white glimmering lights.

"Wow, Dr. Ringle," said Aaron through his mask. "Everything looks fantastic! But you guys are decorating for Christmas a bit early, don't you think?"

"Well Aaron, time is precious on the 5th floor. It's important to the children that we make Christmas last as long as we possibly can. If I could, I'd stretch this Christmas season right on through the next twelve months."

"Why is time precious here?" I asked.

"That's a good question, Mo. In fact, it's something we need to talk about. Do you know what a terminal illness is?" Dr. Ringle looked back and forth between Aaron and I. Aaron nodded that he understood, but I just shook my head. "Well, many of the children on this floor have a type of cancer or other illnesses that are very difficult to treat. Some of them—not all, mind you, but some—will not get well, no matter what we do."

"You mean you can't help them feel better?"

"We try our best, but sometimes nothing we do can take their sickness away. Does that make sense?"

"If you can't help them get better, when do they get to leave the hospital?" I asked, still trying hard to understand.

Recognizing that Dr. Ringle's subtlety wasn't going to cut through my thick layers of naivety, Aaron decided to help out. With a little reluctance he leaned over and whispered a few words into my ear. I'm sure my eyes probably got very wide just then as my mind connected all of the fuzzy dots.

When I spoke again, I intended my words to come out as a

mere whisper only for Aaron and Dr. Ringle to hear, but the effect they had on everyone in the room was more in line with outright shouting. "*You mean all these kids are gonna die!?!?*" That was, in fact, not the case as I would eventually learn. Some of those children would go on to lead long and healthy lives. But the gloomy implication to my tender sensitivities was more or less the same.

If the 5th floor had been moderately quiet before, it was now eerily so. The pounding of my heart, compounded by the penetrating stares of everyone within earshot, amplified the silence until it was deafening. I was grateful for the surgical mask that concealed my identity. It goes without saying that I felt terrible. Indeed, I still feel pangs of remorse to this day for saying those words so loud, but my juvenile mouth couldn't hold back the emotions I felt in that instant when I learned of the likely fate of so many of the young children who stood staring at me.

In those moments of silence, when the world seemed to stand still, each face before me was permanently seared on my memory. With the exception of my funny looking clothes, these children were no different than I. Questions flooded my mind, begging for answers that couldn't be given. *Why should they have to die so young? How long will they live? Why them and not me? Will I get sick and die young, too?*

Dr. Ringle finally broke the silence. "Well, since it seems we have your undivided attention, I'd like to introduce you all to my very special helpers, Aaron and Molar. They are two of the finest elves south, east, or west of the North Pole."

A few of the parents chuckled, others snickered, and that was that. Everyone went back to what they were doing. For many of the children, that meant they were still staring at us as we made our way to a large gathering area filled with tables and chairs. Each table was decked out with colorful table runners and beautiful Christmas centerpieces. At the front of the room was the same velvety throne Dr. Ringle had used at the Santa Shack.

After providing us with a few basic instructions about our role as Santa's official emissaries, Dr. Ringle, in his heavy Scottish tones, gave a heartfelt holler to open the evening's festivities. "Ho!! Ho!! Ho!! And a very Merry Christmas to one and all!"

The children who had been lingering nearby since our arrival were the first to line up to talk to Santa. It was no secret that the man behind the red suit was Dr. Ringle, but each child nevertheless treated him as the one and only St. Nick.

Aaron was asked to hand out candy canes to each of the children after they had spoken with Santa while I was told to give them each a familiar looking red paper just before they stepped forward to the foot of the great red chair. The title at the top of the paper read: *All I Want For Christmas Is. . . .*

The first child in line was a waif of a girl, probably six or seven years old, but her physical frailty made her look younger still. She glided up next to me in pink Barbie pajamas and a pair of fluffy bunny slippers. Atop her head was a cloth wrap which concealed a hairless scalp and several large bandages.

"Hello there," she said precociously. "I'm Rachel."

"Uh . . . hi Rachel," I replied awkwardly. "Have a paper." I pulled the top page from my stack and held it out for her.

"That's it?" she asked. "Have a paper? Aren't you going to tell me your name? Or at least wish me a Merry Christmas? I think it would be nice."

"But," I floundered, "Santa told everyone my name is Mo. Didn't you hear him?"

"Of course I did, silly. I'm not deaf. But it's polite to introduce yourself when someone introduces themselves to you. That's what mother says."

"Right. Sorry. Merry Christmas, Rachel. I'm Mo. It's nice to meet you."

"Much better. Thank you, Molar." She stood smiling expectantly. "I'll take my paper now."

Dr. Ringle was waiting patiently as Rachel slid over to his velvety throne. He sat looking down at her through his thick white beard, his eyes as warm and inviting as they'd ever been. Here at the hospital he didn't bother to use the inflatable belly and legs, but the children didn't seem to mind. All they saw in the red suit was a magical man who was bringing them happiness and joy at a time when they needed it most.

"Hello, Miss Rachel," he said jovially. "How are you tonight?"

"Good, how about you Dr. Ring—I mean Santa?"

"Fine, thank you very much. I see Mo gave you a red paper. That, my dear, is an empty Christmas list. Do you already know what you want for Christmas?"

"Yes!" She said eagerly.

"Oh good. Are there lots of things you'd like from Santa this year?"

"Yes Santa, I want a bunch of stuff!" Rachel's tiny frame shook with delight at the thought of it.

Dr. Ringle paused a moment before speaking again, and when he did his voice was much softer. "Rachel," he said leaning forward. "If I brought you everything you want for Christmas it would be a grand sight to be sure. But this year I would like you to put only one thing on your list. It can be whatever you want, but try to think of something that will bring you more than just a few fleeting moments of fun. Try to think of something that will really make you happy. Can you do that for me?"

"Sure Santa. I can do that."

"Very good. Once you've decided what you want, just bring me back your paper with your name on it. If you're not done tonight, that's fine. My two elves will be here every Monday, Wednesday, and Friday evening until Christmas." He looked up at me briefly and winked.

Below the surgical mask my mouth hung open, but I couldn't muster any words of contradiction. *Every Monday, Wednesday, and Friday night? I thought this was a one time deal!* As much as I wanted to say something, I knew it wouldn't be proper for an elf to question Santa in front of so many children, so I forced my mouth shut.

"So you can give it to one of them on another day if you need," he continued, "and they'll be sure to get it to me at the North Pole. Now go along and get your candy cane and have a Merry Christmas!"

For almost an hour I handed out red papers to the children as they reached the front of the line, then listened as Santa encouraged them all to think of the one thing they'd like more than anything else in the world. After listening excitedly to his counsel they'd trounce off to join their family and write down their one great desire.

Many of the children seemed perfectly healthy to me, but I knew that something must be terribly wrong on the inside for them to be here on floor number five. Some of them had obvious signs of ill-health such as bandages, scars, bruises, and limps. Others were too weak to walk on their own and were pushed in wheelchairs by their parents or the nursing staff. Each one smiled at me bravely as they received their red paper.

By the start of the second hour children began cycling back through to give their single-item lists to Santa Claus.

"Have you decided on that one special thing?" he would ask.

With a nod or a 'yep' they leaned in and whispered the one wish of their heart to the magical man before them, then gave him their red papers. Between the commotion of the large room and the quiet of the whispering voices in Santa's ear, I had trouble making out what most of the kids asked for. But one girl spoke loud enough for everyone to hear that she wanted a trip to Disneyland for her whole family. A boy named Tim, who was pulling around an I.V., nearly shouted that he wanted an Air Jammer Road Rammer.

"Me too!" I squealed. Tim turned to look at me, and I flashed a white latex thumbs-up in honor of his fine choice.

Santa grimaced and reminded me that good elves should keep their holiday wishes to themselves if they hope to get 'everything they've never wanted for Christmas.'

"What does that mean, Santa?" The boy looked baffled. "Why

are you giving him everything he *never* wanted?"

Santa grimaced again then chuckled lightly, shooting me another glance. "Because, Timothy," he said slowly. "Both of these elves would like nothing less for Christmas than everything they could possibly think of. But that would never do for such upstanding elves. So I've decided to give them something even better this year, on account of being such good helpers. The gift they will receive will be better than everything they thought they wanted, but since they didn't think of it on their own, I'm calling it everything they *never* wanted. Does that make sense?"

"I think so," said Timothy. "Does that mean he doesn't get an Air Jammer Road Rammer?"

"Well," he laughed. "I guess we'll have to wait and see. But if all goes as planned he'll be getting something far better."

"Oh." Timothy scratched is head. "Then I'd like to change my list. I want whatever he's getting for Christmas!" Timothy pointed at me.

"Ho! Ho! Ho! I think that's a splendid idea! I can't make any promises, but I'll do my best. Okay, Tim?" Dr. Ringle's eyes were on fire again. "In fact," he said, glancing up at the line of children, "I hope every one of the children at the hospital can get everything they've never wanted for Christmas this year."

CHAPTER

Four

"Until one feels the spirit of Christmas, there is no Christmas. All else is outward display—so much tinsel and decorations."

❁ Author unknown ❁

The line to see Santa thinned down considerably by eight-thirty, and before nine o'clock there was no line at all. When it was clear that everyone who wanted to see Santa had done so, Dr. Ringle took Aaron and I aside.

"You've done a fantastic job tonight. The children have really loved having you here, if nothing else than for something funny to look at!" Dr. Ringle propelled his wheelchair forward as he spoke, then spun it in a circle. "But I have one more job for you this evening. There are two children who didn't come see me tonight. They just stayed by themselves in their rooms. We need to go give them a red paper and a candy cane, too, so they don't feel left out. Aaron, I'll take you with me to meet the first one, then Mo, you'll come with me to meet the other. The next time you boys come back I expect you to retrieve their lists and help them out in any way you can. Okay?"

We both agreed.

Dr. Ringle and Aaron moved to the nearest door, knocked a few times, then vanished as the door closed behind them. I could faintly hear the sounds of chatter from where I stood but couldn't make out any of the particulars.

After a few minutes, Dr. Ringle left the two boys alone to get to know one another. Rolling out in his wheelchair, he led me to a closed room at the far end of the hallway. In comparison to the other doors, this one was noticeably plain. The only thing of interest was a name tag that read *Katrina Barlow, Age 9,* below which hung a crayon-scribbled paper with the words, *E.D. – 12/79.*

Dr. Ringle tapped gently several times before clearing his throat to speak. "Katrina? Ho, Ho, Ho. It's Santa Claus. May I come in? I've brought an elf with me."

"No Dr. Ringle! Don't come in!" shouted a girls voice through the door. "I don't want any visitors now."

"But Kat, it's only me and my elf. We'll just be a minute." There was no reply. For a few seconds there was no sound at all, and then I heard some soft ruffling noises, followed by some shuffling and squeaks. Dr. Ringle was smiling at me. "She's getting ready for us," he whispered. "I think she's going to let us in."

"I can HEAR you Dr. Ringle! What makes you think I'm gonna let you in?"

"Well, I don't know. But it would be an awful tragedy if you didn't get to meet my elf. He's quite a sight you know." Dr. Ringle was still grinning. A few more moments of silence followed.

"Okay," came the reply at last. "Come in—but only for a minute."

Dr. Ringle twisted the doorknob and pushed the heavy door slowly open, then rolled his blinking wheelchair through the doorway. I followed close behind, unsure of what to expect. The only light in the room came from a dim table lamp in the corner near the bed.

Through the shadows that draped the small space in melancholy, I noticed this room was void of holiday decorations. There were no Christmas wreathes on the walls or garland around the bed rails, no ribbons or holly hanging from the ceiling, and no Christmas tree in the windowsill.

In contrast to her sterile surroundings, Katrina herself was an unforgettable sight. Toilet paper had been looped methodically around her limbs and torso like a half finished mummy such that streaks of her bright red pajamas were visible beneath the white wrapping. The only part of her body not bound in toilet tissue was her head, which was completely hidden beneath a white paper bag. A hole for the mouth had been cut out along with two eye holes, through which I could see that she was watching me intently, examining every inch of my colorful outfit.

"Hello Katrina, don't you look lovely tonight," said Dr. Ringle sincerely as he moved to her side. The rubber wheels of his chair squeaked to a halt. "How are you feeling?"

I'm sure she heard his words, but Katrina did not respond. Instead, she continued to focus all of her attention on me. It was several unnerving moments before she said anything, but when she did speak it was not in response to Dr. Ringle's questions.

"So what did they have to pay you to wear *THAT*?" she asked. I couldn't tell if she was joking or serious but hoped it wasn't' the latter.

"Uh . . . nothing," I said lamely. "How about you? Why are you wrapped up in toilet paper? It's Christmas, not Halloween."

"You mean you can't tell? I just . . ." she choked. "I wanted to look like a candy cane." There was more than a hint of disappointment in her voice. The paper bag covering her head slumped forward. "Oh well. It was probably a silly idea anyway. I just didn't want to be the only one not dressed up."

"But . . ." I said slowly as my mind raced to find something to say, some way to take back what had just come out of my overly-honest mouth. "But you *do* look like a candy cane. I was just joking," I lied. "See, I have one right here, and you look just like it!" I stepped quickly forward, holding up the long red and white candy for her to see. "I brought it just for you."

Just then the curly-toed booties that I had struggled with all night finally got the better of me, and I tripped. As I fell to the floor the candy cane flew up in the air in the general direction of Dr. Ringle and Katrina. Dr. Ringle did all he could to stretch out for it, but the confines of his wheelchair prevented him from making a saving catch. The candy cane crashed to the hard tile floor, breaking into countless tiny shards.

From my position on the floor I heard a whimpering cry coming from somewhere beneath the white paper bag that hovered above me. I wasn't sure whether it was the broken candy on the floor or my comments about her costume that ignited the tears, but one thing was certain: I was to blame for *two* shattered candy canes that night. One remained splintered on the cold tiles while the other stood sobbing in coiled fluffy sheets of toilet paper.

"Molar," sighed Dr. Ringle at long last. "I think it is probably time for you and Aaron to go change your clothes. Your father will be here soon. I'll give Katrina the Christmas list and meet you downstairs in a few minutes."

"Yes Santa," I said quietly as I shuffled my way carefully back to the hallway.

I rode the elevator with Aaron down to the first floor and changed out of my elf costume without saying a word. My mind was again full of questions: *What did Katrina look like under the bag?*

Why didn't she visit Santa with the other kids? And why wasn't her room decorated for Christmas? Along with the questions in my head there was also a pit in my stomach, a gut-wrenching regret for what had happened in Katrina's room.

I was busy thinking about it all when Dr. Ringle entered the locker room. He had already taken off his beard and Santa suit, but his red hat still hung from his head.

"I'm sorry about the candy cane," I said immediately.

"I know, lad," he replied. "Accidents do happen sometimes, even for elves."

"And I'm sorry for what I said about Halloween."

"I know." Dr. Ringle did not look up.

"Dr. Ringle, why is Katrina in the hospital? And how long has she been here?"

"I think you should ask her those questions yourself the next time you see her. I told her you'll be coming by on Wednesday to pick up her Christmas list."

"You mean I have to go see her again?" I asked. The last thing on earth I wanted to do was face that girl again after making her cry.

Dr. Ringle just smiled and said, "You'll be fine, Mo. You'll be just fine."

CHAPTER

Five

"Christmas is not a time nor a season, but a state of mind. To cherish peace and goodwill, to be plenteous in mercy, is to have the real spirit of Christmas."

❁ Calvin Coolidge ❁

On the way to the hospital on Wednesday night, I had my mom stop by the grocery store so I could buy the largest candy cane I could find. I paid for it out of my allowance but figured it was worth every cent if it helped show Katrina that I was genuinely sorry for the mess I'd made of everything on my first visit.

Dr. Ringle was not waiting for us when we arrived so Aaron and I made our way to the locker room by ourselves where we found a hand-written letter taped to our locker.

Dear Aaron & Mo,

Thanks again for your help on Monday. I have spoken to the Chief of Staff, and if you would like to go upstairs without the surgical masks and gloves from now on that will be fine, so long as you wash your hands very thoroughly before each visit. Also, you may choose to don the elf costumes if you wish, but it is not mandatory.

I will not be around for a few weeks, as I have some important business to attend to at a Children's Center up north. Please remember to collect any remaining Christmas lists and save them for my return. You have also been granted permission to take part in our annual Christmas Pageant to be held on Christmas Eve. Parts will be handed out this Friday night at 7:00 so don't be late.

Finally, do take the time to get to know Madhu and Katrina. They are your most important assignments while I'm gone!

Sincerely,

Dr. Christoffer K. Ringle, MD

Once we were on the fifth floor and had signed in at the nurses station, we decided to start our evening by making rounds to each of the rooms in search of red papers. Aaron knocked on the first door.

"Come in," came a voice. Opening the door we found a young boy sitting up in bed watching television. I recognized him immediately as Timothy, the boy who wanted the Air Jammer Road Rammer.

"Hi, Tim," I said. "We're the elves who were here the other night with Santa."

"Oh hi!" he replied. "I didn't recognize you without the costumes."

"Yeah," said Aaron. "We felt kinda girly in those tights so we left them downstairs. Anyway, we're just going around trying to collect any Christmas lists that weren't already given to Santa. Do you have one?"

"Nope. I gave mine back to Dr. Ringle. I wanted to make sure he had it before he left for the North Pole."

Aaron and I looked at each other.

"What do you mean? Why would he go to the North Pole?" I asked.

"Well you should know since you work for him. That's where he lives—at the North Pole. Duh, where else would Santa Claus live?" said the boy in all seriousness. Tim folded his arms tightly together across his waist.

Aaron and I traded glances again.

"But he's a doctor. Even you called him *Doctor* Ringle," I responded. "He's just a regular guy."

"Yep. He tells everyone he's just a regular guy. But the nurses say every year he goes away suddenly for several weeks right before Christmas. I heard he goes to the North Pole! And what about his name? You can't say he's not Santa with that name."

"What about his name? Doctor Ringle. It's just a name. Doctor Christoffer K. Ringle." And then, as I repeated the full name aloud I understood what Timothy meant—Dr. Ringle's name *was* suspiciously close to that of Santa's famous alias: Chris Kringle. And he'd written in his note that he was going up north to a Children's center, which confirmed the nurses' stories about annual trips.

Is it possible, I wondered, *that the Children's Center is just a crafty name for the toy factory where he and his elves make toys for children? No way.*

"But . . ." said Aaron. "There's no such thing as a real Santa Claus so it's not worth talking about."

"Right," I agreed tentatively. My brother was wise, I knew, but I still found the parallels perplexing. Even the remote chance that Santa Claus might actually exist was thrilling. "Well, sorry to bother you, Tim, but we've got to go to the other rooms now."

"No bother. Come back any time!" he yelled as we closed the door behind us. "And put in a good word for me with Santa!"

For the next thirty or forty minutes we continued knocking on each of the patients' doors on the fifth floor. Not surprisingly, behind each door we found a child who had already given their list back to Dr. Ringle during the party on Monday night. Still, all of the children were genuinely pleasant and were more than eager to talk with Santa's helpers, even if we lacked the appropriate attire.

In much less time than we would have liked, we finished speaking to almost every child. There remained only two doors, Katrina's and Madhu's. A pit grew in my stomach as I thought of facing Katrina again.

"Let's go to your guy first," I offered. "What's his name again?"

"Madhu. Sounds like 'Mud Who'. His full name is longer, but I can't remember how to say it."

Aaron had met Madhukar Amburi on the previous visit and found him fascinating, if not slightly comical. The door to his room was cracked open a bit, allowing the sound of music to escape from within. It was unlike any music I'd ever heard before. The lyrics were definitely foreign and were sung in a rhythmical chant that throbbed like oriental yodeling.

We knocked hard several times, but the volume of his music was too high for our knocking to be heard. Aaron spoke loudly through the crack.

"Hello? Madhu? Are you in there?"

The music went silent.

"Ohmyyes. Mostdefinitely. Iamverymuchhere. Constantlysoinfact." The words raced out in a phonetic blur.

"What did he say?" I whispered.

Aaron shook his head and whispered back, "Dunno. He talks *REALLY* fast. It takes a few minutes to catch on." Aaron tried speaking through the crack again. "Uh, can we come in?"

"Absolutely," he replied in a flash. Madhu spoke faster than my brain could comprehend. "Ofcourse youcancomein. Mydoor isalwaysopen, asyoucansee. Butwhoareyou exactly? ThatiswhatIamwondering."

We assumed that all of those words boiled down to 'yes' so we pushed the door open and stepped inside. The boy sat at a small desk near the bed. He had a lanky build with dark olive skin and jet black hair. His deep brown eyes reminded me of Dr. Ringle, for they radiated when he smiled.

Following brief, and somewhat misunderstood introductions, we spent a good portion of the next thirty minutes listening to the ebb and flow of Madhu's amazing vernacular. Within a few minutes time my ears adjusted to the inflections and timing of his speech, allowing me to catch at least the gist of what he was talking about.

Madhu was originally from Delhi, India, but had moved with his family to the United States when he was eight. He was a wiry ball of energy who never stopped smiling and seemed to know something clever about everything. I liked him right off and found myself drawn to his amiable personality.

Most remarkable to me was how uncommonly upbeat Madhu was, even about his medical condition. He had been brought to the hospital just one month earlier after tests for liver cancer came up positive. The disease had not spread beyond the liver so there was hope of recovery if the doctors could find a liver donor in time for him to receive a transplant. Time, however, was of the essence because his liver was beginning to show serious signs of failure.

Without a new liver within the next few months, Madhu's hopes of recovery diminished significantly.

Since my brother and I were at the Hospital in conjunction with the holiday season, our conversation with Madhu eventually landed on the subject of Christmas. It was a topic that evoked strong opinions from our new Indian friend even though he had never celebrated the holiday.

"The fact of the matter is," he said as matter-of-factly as he could, "that most of the Christian world does not even understand what they are celebrating at Christmas time. According to everything I've read, Christmas is, at its heart, about Jesus Christ. And yet Santa Claus appears to be the primary figure celebrated in practice. Does that not seem strange to you? It does to me, but I'm not a Christian so my point of view may be skewed. Can you set me straight?"

Aaron tried to respond, but it was hard to argue with Madhu's reasoning. "Well," he said, "Santa Claus was . . . a saint."

By the look on his face, I surmised that the wheels spinning in my brother's head were trying hard to get some sort of traction for wherever he was going next.

"Yeah, a saint," he continued. "He's Saint Nick, right? And everyone knows that saints are Christians who do good things, and . . . and the good thing that Saint Nick does is to bring kids presents. It's all very simple. See?" Even Aaron seemed to question the words he'd just spit out.

"So," said Madhu, quicker than reindeer feet on a cold Christmas night, "what you are saying is that Christmas is only about Santa bringing Christian children rewards and by so doing has qualified himself for sainthood. Is that it? That is most interesting." His sarcastic tone suggested he wasn't buying Aaron's explanation.

"Yes," muttered Aaron. "I mean, no. It's just that. I mean . . . I dunno what I mean."

Madhu didn't want to trivialize Christmas through his persistent questioning. Nor did he want to contend with our beliefs. Rather, he genuinely wanted to know why Christmas was so important to us and how Santa fits into the picture, given that the stated cause for the celebration was the birth of Jesus Christ.

As the two older boys sat analyzing what the other had said, it donned on me that there was, perhaps, a potential connection between the modern-day Santa and baby Jesus.

"Hey, I got it!" I shouted.

"Got what?" asked Madhu.

"I think I know why Santa is part of Christmas and why he gives gifts. Maybe he was a wise guy!"

"What are you talking about?" Aaron asked.

"You know, the three wise guys! He was probably one of them

that brought Jesus gifts when he was born."

"Those were the wise *men*," Aaron snorted. "They followed the star from the east. Why would he be one of them?"

"I was just thinking that maybe after bringing baby Jesus a special gift he decided to keep giving gifts to children every year as a way for us all to remember."

"Well I'm not very familiar with the story," said Madhu thoughtfully. He was rubbing his chin with his index finger as he stared at me. "But, if what you say *were* true, it would make more sense than anything else I've heard about Santa Claus." He winked and smiled at Aaron.

"Well if you think his idea is so interesting, you should join the Christmas pageant with us." Aaron sounded only slightly miffed that Madhu favored my explanation of Santa Claus more than his own. "I bet they'd let you be one of the Wise Men, and that way you could learn all you want about them."

"Yes, most definitely! That is a wonderful suggestion Aaron. I would very much like to learn about the men from the east who were wise."

That settled it. Madhu would join us in the pageant.

The only other mention of Christmas during our time with him that night was when we asked him about his Christmas list. To our surprise, he'd already ripped up the infamous red paper and thrown it away in the garbage, claiming that the thing he wanted most in the world was not within Santa Claus' power to give. He also said that even if Santa *could* give him what he wanted, he probably wouldn't because Madhu is not Christian. I didn't think that was right but didn't press the matter.

When it came time to end our visit with Madhu, I secretly wished we could stay there and listen to him chatter away just a little bit longer, partly because I was dreading our final stop of the evening. I knew from experience that Katrina was nothing like Madhu. While he had been happy, she would be sad. Where he found the positive, she positively would not.

"Hello," I said quietly as I knocked on Katrina's door, half hoping that I wouldn't be heard. "Katrina, its Molar, the elf from the other night. Are you in there?"

"Don't come in!" she shouted loud enough for the whole floor to hear. "I don't want visitors!"

"Wow," said Aaron under his breath. "She's got some serious lungs. At least we know she's here."

"I can HEAR you, you know! And of course I'm here. Where else would I be? I'm not dead yet!"

This was already starting off worse than I'd feared. "Dr. Ringle lied," I whispered softly back to my brother. "He said this would go fine. She doesn't seem too. . . ."

"Hey! I can still hear you! If you're going to talk about me, at least do it to my face you no good, clumsy servant of Santa!"

We stood there for a few awkward moments, not sure whether to run and hide or just keep trying. If not for a promise made to Dr. Ringle that I would retrieve her Christmas list, I probably would have turned and walked back to Madhu's room right then and forgotten all about Miss Katrina Barlow. But a promise is a promise.

"Uh, okay," I ventured. "Is that an invitation to come in?"

"What?" she retorted sharply.

"You said to come say it to your face. Can we . . . ummm . . . come in and talk to you then?"

"That's not what I meant. I meant you should just be quiet."

"I know," I admitted. "But can we come in anyway? My brother is here with me this time, and we really want to talk to you."

It was silent for a few minutes. Then we head some soft ruffling noises followed by some shuffling and squeaks. I knew from my first visit that those noises were a good sign that she was getting ready for us, but I didn't dare tell Aaron, lest she should hear me and change her mind. After another minute or two of silence, she finally spoke again, this time in a much nicer tone.

"Okay. You may come in—but only for a minute."

Since I'd already met Katrina before, if only long enough to make her start crying, Aaron insisted that I lead the way into the room. With every ounce of caution that I possessed, I carefully pulled the extra-large candy cane from the inside pocket of my coat and held it high in front of me, like a torch lighting my way, then gently pressed the door open and inched forward.

"I've uh . . . I've brought you something, Katrina," I said as my hand crossed the threshold, each finger holding tightly to the red and white striped peace offering that I carried. "It's bigger than the other candy. . . ." My words cut off mid-sentence, and my feet froze in place as I looked up and saw Katrina standing where she had before against the opposite wall. Gone were the red pajamas wrapped in toilet paper, but she was still wearing the white paper bag over her head. I swallowed hard. "Katrina, is that a . . . another costume?"

"You mean the bag? No you dope!" she fired. "It wasn't part of my candy cane costume either!"

"Then why are you wearing it?" asked Aaron as he stepped to my side.

"Are you serious? I guess my grandpa was right. He always used to say, 'there's no such think as a dumb question, only dumb people'. How about you take a guess, Mr. Genius?" Much to my relief, she was looking at Aaron. "Why do you suppose I have a bag on my head?"

I couldn't see the expression on her face because the bag covered it up, but her tone made it clear that this was a touchy subject.

"Umm. . . ," Aaron muttered. "Maybe because your hair was messed up and you couldn't find a hat to cover it?"

"Wrong-o! How about you Candy Man?" Now she was glaring at me.

I lowered the candy cane as I weighed what I might say, but there were no good options. I knew full well that whatever I said would be wrong.

"You . . . you probably have some bandages you don't want us to see until they heal. Right?"

"Wrong again! You want to know why I have a bag on my head?"

It was a rhetorical question that required no formal response, but we both nodded our heads anyway while Katrina took a long pause. I could see through the eye holes in the bag that she was no longer looking at us but was staring down at the ground. She took a big sigh, perhaps to release some anger before she exploded.

"It's," she started again as her shoulders slumped forward. Her voice was barely audible. "It's because I'm ugly. I wasn't ugly before the cancer and all the treatments and stuff, you know. Now nobody would want to look at me without the bag. *I* don't even like to look at me."

I wanted to say something that would help her feel better, but I couldn't come up with a single word. Later that night in bed, as I laid awake reenacting the scene over and over in my head, I would fire off countless perfect things I should've said to Katrina, but in the heat of the moment my mind was shooting blanks. Aaron and I both just stood there, watching the girl cry behind the wrinkled white of her paper bag.

Once is bad enough. Now I'm two-for-two at making this girl cry! What kind of elf am I?

After what felt like an eternity, Katrina finally lifted up her eyes and said the words I desperately wanted to hear.

"Please go," she said.

We went.

CHAPTER

Six

"Our hearts grow tender with childhood memories and love of kindred, and we are better throughout the year for having, in spirit, become a child again at Christmas-time."

❁ Laura Ingalls Wilder ❁

Friday night, December 5th, was the designated evening for assigning parts in the annual Christmas Pageant, and most of the children were noticeably chipper when we arrived. Many of them now knew us by name and greeted us as we made our way through the hallway to Madhu's room.

His door swung open just as we were about to knock.

"Hello elves!" he said when he saw us. "You are here fetching me for the pageant, are you not?"

"Yes," chuckled Aaron. "We are *fetching*. Ready to go?"

"Oh my yes. Very much so. I can't wait to learn more about the wise guys . . . er . . . men from the east. I have been studying a little on my own."

"That's great," said Aaron as he and Madhu turned to head back up the hallway toward the designated rehearsal room.

As they walked away, a thought crept into my head which kept me firmly planted in place. "Hey guys," I called after them. "I wonder if . . . well, should we invite Katrina to come?"

"You mean Katrina with the paper bag?" asked Aaron.

As much as I dreaded facing the girl again, something inside said it wouldn't be right if we didn't at least try. "Well, yeah. It's just, I don't want her to feel left out. You know?"

"That would be splendid," said Madhu, and he sounded like he genuinely meant it. "I've met this girl of which you speak. I'm sure she would be happy to join us."

Aaron laughed again. "Are you sure we're talking about the same girl?"

The three of us walked down the hall to Katrina's door and then democratically decided that Madhu should be the spokesperson.

Madhu smiled brightly as he knocked on the door. "Hello Katrina, it's your Indian neighbor from just several meters down the hall. I'm the boy who is from India, not the girl who is native American, but who everyone refers to as the Indian. Remember me?"

As usual, Madhu was talking at break-neck speed, and I wondered whether she'd be able to understand what he was saying. He didn't pause or take a break between thoughts. It was more like a gushing stream of consciousness.

"But of course you remember me," he continued without

waiting for a response. "Yes, most definitely! How can one forget the only boy in the entire hospital who does not celebrate Christmas? Katrina, are you there? May we come in? Hello?"

"Are the two boys with you?" she said without her normal silent pause. "The elf boys?"

"Oh yes, yes! Absolutely. The elves have returned again, from the North Pole, I think." I couldn't be sure, but I thought I heard a small giggle from somewhere behind the door. "They are standing here beside me and are interested in how you are doing. May we come in?"

"Yes, just give me a second."

Aaron and I were shocked at the warm reception. It only took a few moments of shuffling sounds before she shouted that we could enter. As I moved through the doorway my eyes fell again on the crayon-drawn sign below Katrina's nameplate.

"Hi Katrina. What does this mean?" I asked before the question slipped my mind. "E.D. Twelve. Seventy-Nine," I said, reading the inscription aloud. "Is that a special date or something?"

"Sort of," she said through her bag as she walked around from the other side of the bed. "It's when I was supposed to die, last December. The E. D. stands for Estimated Death."

"Oh," I said, wishing I hadn't been so nosey. "Sorry."

"That's alright. It just helps me remember to be thankful for every day. The doctors all told me I probably wouldn't live to see last Christmas, and I'm still here."

I didn't like to hear about dying so I changed the subject as fast as I could.

"Do you still have the red Christmas list from Dr. Ringle?" I blurted out. "I'm supposed to get it back for him."

"Oh, I already gave it to him," she said.

"You did?" I was more than a bit surprised to hear that. "But he told me to come get it from you. When did you give it to him?"

"On the night we met. I was pretty mad that night because, well, you know, what with the candy cane and all. Once you were gone he gave me the paper, and I wrote down what I wanted. Then I wadded it up in a ball and threw it right back at him. It hit him square in the nose!"

"Perhaps," Madhu interjected, "Dr. Ringle misplaced your list, Katrina. That is certainly a possibility."

"Right," added Aaron. "He probably lost it. How about you write it down again for us?"

"No way. You'll look at it! I don't want anyone but Santa to see my list. Besides, I already gave it to him once, and that should be good enough."

"Suit yourself, but don't blame us elves if you don't get what you want for Christmas," I said jokingly, but she didn't think it was very funny.

Crossing her arms she shot back at me in a voice that was closer to her usual self. "I *KNOW* I'm not getting it for Christmas anyway! Santa can't give me what I want. I shouldn't have even bothered writing it down on that stupid paper."

Madhu didn't seem bothered by Katrina's quick change in temperament. In his typical upbeat way he squelched the fire that was starting to burn with a few speedy words.

"Well then," he said, "that makes two of us who are *definitely* not getting anything for Christmas. Your list is lost, maybe in one of Dr. Ringle's nostrils if you threw it hard enough, while mine was ripped to shreds by a crazy Indian boy and sent out with the trash."

Katrina laughed at that. It was probably the first time in a long time that laughter had escaped her white paper disguise.

"Katrina," I said as the chuckles subsided. "We didn't just come here to get your list. We're going tonight to get parts in the Christmas pageant and were wondering if you'd like to come? It's gonna be fun to be. . . ."

"No," she said before I even finished speaking. Her tone and body language had changed again without warning.

"But Katrina," chimed Aaron. "We thought you might like . . ."

"Didn't you hear me?" she asked nastily. "No means no."

Silence followed. I didn't dare open my mouth again for fear of what Katrina might do or say if I did. Aaron, too, kept quiet while Madhu paced slowly around the room, seemingly in deep thought. Katrina stood firm, her eyes darting back and forth between the three of us.

Finally Madhu broke the silence.

"I have an idea!" he shouted as he turned to face the pair of green eyes glaring out through the paper bag. "Katrina, I've heard you used to participate in the gurney races. Is that true?"

"Yes," she replied questioningly. "But I stopped going. Too many kids made fun of me. Besides, nobody could beat me so the thrill of it was gone."

"I can beat you," Madhu said, still looking her straight in the eyes.

I didn't know what gurney races were, but if Madhu could race as fast as he could speak, I figured he could beat just about anyone.

"*Nobody* can beat me," she snarled as she planted her hands on her hips. "Cuz' I'm not afraid of getting hurt. I'm going to die soon anyway."

"Then race me!" Madhu was smiling nonchalantly. "If you win, then we forget all about the Christmas Pageant—none of us will participate. But if I win, then you must come with us and take whatever part you are assigned. Deal?"

Katrina didn't respond immediately. She seemed to be sizing up her challenger. "No," she said finally.

"But Katrina!" Madhu fired back. "If you think you can't be beat, then why. . . ."

Katrina cut him off mid-sentence. "I'll race him!" She was pointing in my direction.

I looked back over my shoulder on the off chance that someone had snuck up behind me. There was nobody there. "If *the little elf* wins, I'll be in the pageant."

Gulp.

❖ ❖ ❖

With so much else going on at the hospital that night it wasn't hard for us to slip unnoticed to the service elevator located on the east corner of the building. It was the only elevator that still serviced the 8th floor during construction, and it was conveniently out of sight from anyone who might have prevented us from going through with what I was beginning to think was a very bad idea.

Gurney races, I soon discovered, were not so much races of speed as they were acts of downright stupidity. Yes, they were fast, but speed was of less importance than distance. It was, more or less, a game of chicken on a hospital gurney. Two competitors climbed aboard their own rolling cart near the top of a long, wide access ramp which sloped gently down towards an open stairwell. It wasn't a steep slope, but the smooth wheels picked up enough velocity on the hard tile floor that by the time racers approached the landing above the stairs they were moving at a dangerous pace. The winner of the race was the one who jumped off the gurney last.

Several children had received moderate injuries as a result of participation in the gurney races, but each had made up a story to the doctors about how they'd been hurt in order to cover up what was going on late at night on floor number eight.

The so-called races had begun in September when the hospital's top floor was closed for renovations. A couple nights each week scores of thrill-seeking patients would sneak upstairs after most of the doctors and nursing staff had gone home for the night. There, beyond the scrutiny of adult supervision, they were free to do as they pleased—and what pleased them the most was racing the gurneys.

❁ ❁ ❁

"You sure about this Katrina?" I asked once we had selected our gurneys and were ready to begin.

From the top of the hallway looking down I felt more than a

little anxiety about our chosen means to get Katrina to participate in the pageant.

"Maybe there's some other competition we could try," I offered hopefully. "A paper airplane contest would be nice."

"Sounds like you're scared, Molar," she said, egging me on. "Are you chicken?"

Even though I was one, I would never admit it. "Yeah, uh huh. As if." It was a lame comeback, I know, but I was too scared to come up with anything better.

"Fine," she said. "Just remember you can't touch the walls to slow yourself down, otherwise you are disqualified. And you have to stay head-first on your stomach until you jump off. Got it?"

"Yeah," I chirped. "Let's just get this over with so we can go sign up for the Christmas Pageant."

Madhu and Aaron stood holding on behind the gurneys, preventing them from rolling away until we were ready to start the race. Next to me, laying rigid on her stomach, Katrina's green eyes poked through her paper bag as she focused intently on the hallway ahead.

"Okay then, very good. I think we're all set," announced Madhu. "Both of you, please be careful. Mo, if you would be so kind as to win, that would be splendid. I am very anxious to become a wise man." He slapped me on the back for encouragement. "Okay racers, take your mark. Get set. Go!"

As the last word escaped Madhu's lips, he and Aaron gently released our racing machines, allowing gravity to take hold completely. It started out somewhat slowly, and for a second or two I half imagined the race was no big deal.

I was wrong.

Over the next thirty feet the speed picked up considerably, and by fifty feet the wheels of my gurney began wobbling unnaturally under the stress. Katrina and I were literally neck-and-neck, each of us with our head stretched out in front of our accelerating death-traps to better see the approaching stairwell. The bag over Katrina's head soon began flapping in resistance to the air, and for an instant I thought it might catch a breeze and pop right off.

We reached the hundred-foot mark in what seemed like a blur, but the final fifty feet felt more like a slow motion movie. In those remaining seconds I saw pictures of children hanging on the wall, a doctor's stethoscope collecting dust on a cabinet, and even a small wad of gum stuck in a corner where the wall met the floor. But mostly I just saw Katrina next to me, and she showed no signs of giving up. All of my muscles were flexed, ready to spring the instant she made a move to get off.

That moment never came.

With twenty feet left before the edge of the stairs I panicked and screamed out, "Jump!!"

"You first!" she shouted back.

"No you firrrrssssstttt!!!!"

After that it was just screaming and flailing as our rolling beds both hit a lip of carpet near the top-most stair, sending us catapulting head first toward an open landing twenty steps below. On the way down I thought I heard voices shouting from somewhere far behind us, but that was just white noise behind the clamor of steel beds tumbling down the stairs and the terror coming from my own mouth as the concrete floor approached.

"Uggghhh!" My whole body shuttered on impact. For a moment or two I thought I was all right until the world around me started to become gray. Through the fog that enveloped me I saw two bright green eyes staring down at me, hovering somewhere in the mist. The eyes were familiar, yet somehow different then I'd remembered them.

No Bag! I see her face! Is she okay?

And then everything went black.

CHAPTER

Seven

"The greatest mistake in the treatment of diseases is that there are physicians for the body and physicians for the soul, although the two cannot be separated."

❁ Plato ❁

"Mo. Hello? Can you sit up straight please and look at me?" Someone was talking to me, but I didn't recognize the voice. "Mo, try opening your eyes."

"Ah!" I gasped as I followed the instructions. "That's bright!" I brushed my hand instinctively at the small brilliant flashlight that was shining back and forth between my eyes.

"Look up. Good. Look to the left. Good. Yes, I think he has a pretty good concussion to go along with everything else, but that's not surprising given how far he fell. Some aspirin and a few days rest will help that."

When the flashlight clicked off and my pupils returned to normal, I was better able to get my bearings. I was propped up on a hospital bed wearing nothing more than a loose-fitting gown that was completely open down the back. My left arm was held tightly in a sling. Mom and Dad were in the room, along with Aaron and

Madhu, all of them watching attentively as the doctor examined my aching body.

"You're quite lucky, Molar," the doctor said as he kicked his rolling stool away from my bed, then stood and began scribbling notes on a medical chart.

I didn't like how the doctor spoke to me. His voice was a bit nasal, and he articulated his words way too much. When his mouth wasn't moving he scrunched up his lips awkwardly as if he was annoyed at something. Even as a young boy I guessed that he thought way too much of himself.

He didn't look up from his chart as he continued speaking. "A scaphoid fracture of the wrist, middle ribs five through seven fractured at the posterior angle, and a severely bruised clavicle. But other than that just the contusions on your head and face. Not bad really, considering the nature of your . . . eh hum . . . *accident.*"

"Where is Katrina?" I asked once the doctor finished speaking words that were way above my contused head. "Is she okay?

"That's the girl who wears the paper bag, right?" asked Dad. "She's just fine, Son. A few bumps and bruises, but nothing serious. She's in her room. I think she feels bad."

"Why would she feel bad?"

"Well, as near as we can tell, most of your injuries are because of her. We think you broke your wrist on your own, but the other injuries were likely from her landing on you. You hit the ground a split second before she did and broke her fall."

"Yes, that is definitely the case, Mo!" added Madhu excitedly. "Oh, you should've seen it. Truly a spectacle! Something I will never be forgetting in all my days."

"I'm glad *you* enjoyed it," I winced. "But did I win? Is Katrina going to be in the Christmas Pageant?"

I tried to stand up, but a pain in my side told me I should sit still.

"She hasn't decided," shrugged Aaron. "Says she didn't lose since you touched the ground first, even if it was well beyond the finish line. You'll have to talk to her about it."

"But that will have to be another night, I'm afraid," said my mom from her seat in the corner of the room. Surprisingly, she smiled as she talked. "For now, we need to go get a cast on that arm and then get you home."

"So you're not mad at me?"

"Oh, I'm plenty upset," she feigned. "But Aaron and his friend explained why you did it. Mo, we bring you here to spend time helping others. I'm not happy that you put yourself at risk, but I'm proud that you went to such great lengths to try to get Katrina to join the pageant. She seems like she could use a friend like you.

But next time be a little more careful, okay?"

"Okay Mom," I said, trying to hide my smile. "I love you."

A nurse helped me out of bed and rolled me in a wheelchair down to a lab on the first floor where I got my very first cast. It was a heavy, white plaster wrap that extended from the middle of my palm to just beyond my elbow, effectively locking the arm uncomfortably in a right-angle to keep my wrist and forearm better immobilized. My chest was taped and wrapped in an ace bandage. Someone had already stitched my forehead and scalp before I woke up, so there were bandages encircling my head. And the bruised clavicle was more of a tender nuisance than anything else, so after it was iced they left it alone.

By the time the doctors and nurses were done working on me it was nearly eleven o'clock, P.M., and I was very tired and sore. Mom and Dad drove me home and carried me to my bed. I fell asleep as soon as my head hit the pillow.

The week following my gurney accident was perhaps the most mind-numbing expanse of my life. My body hurt too much to move about, and there was very little to do from the confines of my bed. The first day or so was made bearable by cartoons and prescription drugs, but after that I wanted to pull my hair out from boredom (if only my hair was accessible beneath the bandages). Not only did I long to join my brother on the hospital visits in the evenings, but I even missed going to school.

While I was at home in bed, Madhu and Aaron both got parts in the Christmas pageant, even though they missed the first session on account of me getting hurt. Aaron was assigned to be the narrator, a part usually given to one of the nurses, but they made an exception once they heard how well he read the script. Madhu got a part as a wise man, just as he had planned, although it took some strong arm-twisting since all the wise men had been assigned earlier.

"Just imagine it!" said Aaron excitedly when he told me about it later. "A Hindu using the bible to prove he should get a part as a wise man. It was fantastic!"

In order to get his desired role, Madhu discussed the matter with the pageant director, Nurse Wimble from the third floor. She was a quirky woman with big hair and a strong southern accent, and the hospital's self-proclaimed authority on the Bible if only because her husband was an ordained minister. When Madhu explained that he wanted to be one of the Wise Men, she merely laughed thinking he must joking. But when she realized he was serious she flat out refused.

"We already have three Wise Men. We can't have any more

than that," she said indignantly in a long Mississippi drawl.

"But why can't we have more than three? Is there a limit on the number of wise persons who can participate in the Christian story of Jesus' birth?" Madhu tried to talk slowly so the nurse could understand.

"Mr. Am-bu-ri, I know you're not terribly familiar with our religion, but *I* am. I have read the Holy Bible every day for as long as I can remember, and it clearly says there were three wise men. And so that is how many we will have in our production."

"But Nurse Wimble, I am thinking you are wrong." Madhu usually used a lot of words when he spoke, but he also had a way of getting right to the point when he wanted to. He spoke loud enough for people nearby to hear, and they all stopped what they were doing to listen.

"What did you say young man?" snapped the nurse. She was wriggling her nose in disgust. "Are you calling me a liar?"

"Nurse Wimble, I would not be so bold as to say something like that. No, you are definitely not a liar. You are simply mistaken on this matter. The Bible is not specific concerning the total number of wise men."

"It most certainly is! And that is the end of this debate. Now tell me, Mr. Madhu, your people believe the cow is sacred, right? Well holy cow! I just had a wonderful idea! You're gonna be a cow in this here pageant. How does that sound to you?"

"With all due respect, I really prefer to be a wise man."

As he spoke, Madhu pulled out a copy of the Bible from his jacket pocket. It had the name Gideon printed in bold letters on the front cover.

"I read last night in Matthew chapter two, and it states: 'Behold, there came wise men from the east to Jerusalem, saying, Where is he that is born King of the Jews? For we have seen his star in the east, and are come to worship him.' It does not say, or even imply, there were three. But it definitely affirms they were from the east. Yes, on that point the text is clear. I, too, am from the east and would very much like your permission to be the fourth wise man in your pageant."

Nurse Wimble looked around at the gathering crowd, who all appeared very anxious to see how she would respond.

"But . . . there were only three gifts," she whined. "Gold, frankincense, and myrrh. Three gifts and three wise men. What on earth would a fourth wise man bring the Savior anyway?"

"Nurse Wimble, I assure you if I am allowed to be a wise man in your pageant, I will think of a most wonderful gift indeed to give to your baby Jesus!"

It was clear she did not want to allow such a change, but Nurse Wimble finally consented, making Madhu the first fourth wise man in the history of the Children's Hospital annual Christmas Pageant. Now all he had to do was think of a gift.

❖ ❖ ❖

It was Monday, December 15, before I was allowed to go back to visit the children at the hospital, though I was hampered by my cast and head bandages.

Dr. Ringle was still out of town, but Christmas was in full-swing at the hospital even without his jolly presence. Aaron and Madhu had tried to visit Katrina during the week I was absent, but she wouldn't let them in no matter how hard they tried. So my first visit of the evening was to her room while Aaron and Madhu went off to a rehearsal for the pageant.

"Katrina, are you in there?" I said as I knocked lightly on the door.

"Yes. Is that you Molar?"

"Yep," I replied.

"How's your arm?"

"My arm is fine. It' just everything else that hurts," I joked.

"I'm sorry."

"You don't have to be sorry. Can I just come in so we don't have to talk through the door?"

"Just a minute." There was a light shuffling sound like ruffling paper, and then she opened the door. She was wearing a new pair of pajamas and a pair of pink slippers, plus the usual white paper bag to cover her head.

Over the next thirty minutes I got to know Katrina better than I'd thought possible. For the first time she opened up and began to talk about herself, sharing some things that were sad and difficult for me to hear but important for me to understand. The conversation began mild enough with a few laughs about our brush with death on the gurneys, but then it took a more serious turn.

"Katrina, how come you don't talk about your sickness?" I asked. "I don't even know what kind of cancer you have?"

"I used to talk about it more when Grandpa was around. He made me feel better. He always told me everything would be fine." A new sadness reverberated in her words.

"Did he, you know . . . die?" I asked.

She told me he had died four months earlier of a heart attack, and that now she was a ward of the state under the immediate care of the hospital for medical treatment. She never knew her father—even her mother wasn't fully sure who the father was—and tragically, a drunk driver killed her mother on the way to work when Katrina was four years old. So for nearly as long as she could remember she had depended on her grandfather for everything, especially after she was diagnosed with a brain tumor in July of 1979.

As she recounted the horrific details of her life, I couldn't help but reflect on how good my own life was. It was a thought I'd never considered before, that there were people far less fortunate than myself. I realized that I had things *really* easy. I had people who loved me, parents who cared for me, and friends who took interest in me and wanted to associate with me. Katrina had none of that. All she ever had was a fading memory of a mother and a grandfather who she now missed more than anything in the world.

"Grandpa didn't care what I looked like," she said at one point. "He just loved me. I always knew he loved me no matter what. Other people aren't that way."

"Katrina, I'm sorry about your grand-dad and your mom, too."

"Thank you, Molar. I guess not having my grandpa around is why I wouldn't let anyone put up Christmas decorations this year. He always used to love doing that with me, and I'd hate for him to think I was enjoying Christmas without him."

"It's Mo," I corrected. "My friends call me Mo."

"What?"

"My friends call me Mo," I repeated. "You said Molar."

"So I can call you that?" she asked timidly, almost doubting that someone would ever be willing to count her as a friend.

"Of course you can. I wouldn't have it any other way." I can't be sure, but I thought I glimpsed the trace of a smile spreading across her face through the mouth hole in her large paper bag.

"Mo," she said proudly. "I've decided something. Even though I technically didn't lose the gurney race, I didn't exactly win either. So I'm going to keep our bargain and join the Christmas Pageant."

"Really!?" I would have jumped out of my seat, but the lingering pain in my ribs kept me restrained.

"Really, really. Do you think they still have a part for me?"

"I'm sure they do. And if they say they don't, we'll just have Madhu talk to Nurse Wimble for you!"

CHAPTER

Eight

"Christmas began in the heart of God. It is complete only when it reaches the heart of man."

❁ Author Unknown ❁

When we entered the large rehearsal room, the first thing I heard was Aaron. He was standing near the edge of a make-shift stage shouting his lines into the corn dog he was using as a microphone.

"And Joseph also went up from Galilee, out of the city of Nazareth, into Judea, unto the city of David, which is called Bethlehem, to be taxed with Mary his espoused wife, being great with child!"

Nurse Wimble was seated on a chair directly in front of the stage giving directions as fast as her southern twang would allow.

"Okay Mary and Joseph, I want you to look tired, very tired. Especially you Mary! Remember, this ain't no walk in the park, y'all! And hold your belly like this."

The girl playing the part of Mary nodded and wrapped her hands around the pillow she was using as a stomach.

"Donkey? Where's our donkey?" bellowed Nurse Wimble.

"C'mon," I said to Katrina, grabbing her by the shirt with my good arm. "Let's get you a part!"

Katrina dragged her feet a bit as we went, but we still managed to make our way up to the stage. Many of the children stopped to look as we approached. They had all seen Katrina and her bag plenty of times before, but it was clear they still weren't completely comfortable with her appearance. Nor were they accustomed to seeing me with my head wrapped in bandages and my arm in a cast. The sight of us brought a new quiet over the crowd.

"Uhhmm hi, Miss Wimble," said Katrina softly once the nurse stopped barking at the kids on the stage who were watching us instead of listening to her. "I was wondering if you had room in the pageant for one more?"

"I'm sorry, Katrina, but your friend has already been told he cannot participate on account of his injuries. We wouldn't want him falling off the stage or something terrible like that in his current condition."

"Oh no, mam," I interjected. "She's not asking for me. Katrina wants to be in your play."

"Oh I see," she said curtly. "Well, I'm afraid there are simply no more parts available. I suppose one could say there's no more room at this particular inn." She laughed openly at what she thought was a brilliant, if not callous, play on words.

Some of the children on stage snickered and whispered too, and I heard Katrina's name used several times along with the words '*stupid bag*'. I suppose some of them were glad there was, according to Nurse Wimble, no room for Katrina.

"But Nurse Wimble," I protested. "I'm sure there are lots of parts she could do real well!"

By the look in Katrina's eyes she had already given up and would have much preferred that we not push the matter any further, but I didn't think it was fair so I just kept on talking.

"She promised me she'd be in the pageant, and if you don't let her than she'll be breaking a promise. There must be something she can do! You must need more of *something*."

Nurse Wimble made a huffy noise through her nose in contempt.

"Well, does anyone have any ideas?" she asked. "Can anybody think of a part that is suited to our little Katrina?"

Sadly, no one said anything. I looked around frantically, hoping someone would come up with a part—any part—for Katrina, but the silence continued. Finally, just as Nurse Wimble was crossing her arms to settle the matter, a familiar voice piped up.

"Nurse Wimble, I think it would be a most excellent idea if we added a fifth wise man—or wise woman as the case may be—to the Christmas Pageant." Madhu was grinning mischievously as he spoke.

"Absolutely not!" she hollered. "Four is already one more than I should have allowed, Mr. Amburi. But thank you ever so kindly for the suggestion. *Anyone* else?"

Again, silence followed.

"Well then, I'm afraid Katrina will not. . . ."

"An Angel!" a voice shouted from the stage. It was my brother, still yelling into his half-eaten microphone. "She should be an angel. We can never have too many of those!"

Amid the lingering echo of Aaron's suggestion, one particularly snide girl with curly brown hair, who was part of the angel chorus, added her two small cents under her breath, which happened to be just loud enough for everyone to hear.

"An angel?" she scoffed. "With that bag she looks more like the Holy Ghost to me!"

Nearly everyone laughed. Even Nurse Wimble chuckled out loud at the ridiculous comment. Katrina's eyes burned with humiliation as the crowd continued their shameless jeers. Here they all were, practicing a pageant about Jesus Christ, yet completely ignoring the fact that they were behaving completely un-Christ-like.

Aaron, Madhu, and myself stood helpless, wondering what else we could do to help our bag-headed friend out of this most cruel circumstance. Katrina turned, her shoulders slumped and shaking, and began to walk away. I turned to follow, but was stopped by another voice yelling above the ruckus of the crowd.

"I quit!" It was a girl's voice screaming at the top of her lungs.

I turned back to the stage to see a beautiful girl standing beside the manger, yanking a pillow out from beneath her costume. Her name was Lynn, and she had been awarded the lead role of Mary, mother of Jesus. Her eyes were on fire, and I couldn't help but notice how delightfully determined she was as she strode forward to face Nurse Wimble.

"I quit," she said again, pulling the remainder of her costume over her head and tossing it at the feet of the director.

"But you *can't* quit," said Nurse Wimble. "You're the only one who can manage to sing the solos."

"Well that's just too bad," she said. "This hospital is supposed to be a place where we are all cared for, and where we look out for and support one another. I'm sick about the way you all treat Katrina, and I won't stand for it anymore. If there is no room at the inn for her, then there is no room at the inn for me either."

Katrina was practically glowing with gratitude and admiration as she stared up at Lynn. It was the first time that another patient had stood up for her in public, and it gave her spirits a much needed boost.

"Very well," said Nurse Wimble, breaking the silence. "If you'll kindly put your costume back on, we can probably see fit to find a place for Katrina. Besides," she backpedaled, "Aaron was right; we can never have too many angels. Katrina, you'll join that group over there, and they'll tell you what to do. Alright?"

Katrina nodded with excitement.

"Now then," she said through a forced smile, "let's pick up where we left off, shall we?"

Surprisingly, everyone continued on as though nothing had happened. Once Katrina had been introduced to the angel chorus all else was forgotten.

I sat watching the practice for the remainder of the evening, which was more interesting than I had expected. The highlight of the rehearsal came when the innkeeper, played by a short redheaded boy with bright freckles, tripped on his own crutch while trying to walk and read his lines at the same time. He ended up landing on top of a little girl who was supposed to be a sheep in the stable. Fortunately, no one was hurt. However, the little girl was nibbling on a ham sandwich while she waited for her scene to begin, and when the innkeeper fell, the sandwich was inadvertently hurled towards Mary and Joseph, who were hovering in awe over their baby-doll Jesus. Joseph took the brunt of the incident when one mustardy slice of bread hit him in the face then slid off and dropped to his shoe. At the same time, a juicy piece of ham and the other slice of bread plopped squarely down on top of the doll in the middle of the manger.

Aaron, who was still chewing his last bite of corn dog, ad-libbed a quick line into his script.

"And when Mary and Joseph looked upon the babe in swaddling clothes," he said in an artificially deep voice, "they saw that he was hungry, and they did feed him ham on rye."

Everyone laughed. Everyone, that is, except Nurse Wimble.

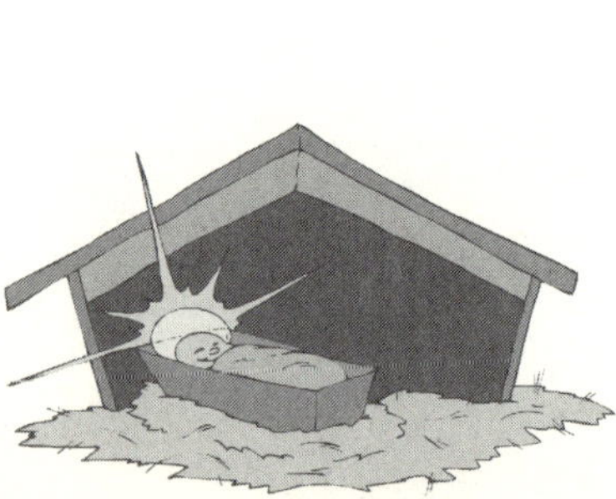

CHAPTER

Nine

"Yes . . . there is a Santa Claus . . . Thank God! He lives, and he lives forever. A thousand years from now . . . , nay ten times ten thousand years from now, he will continue to make glad the heart of childhood."

❁ Francis Pharcellus Church "The Sun" Sept 21, 1897 ❁

With only one week left before Christmas Eve, much of our remaining time at the Children's Hospital centered around practicing for the Christmas Pageant. At least that was the case for Katrina, Madhu, and Aaron, who were fortunate enough to participate. I was forced to find other activities to fill my time, because as soon as Nurse Wimble began her rehearsals, she scooted me unceremoniously out the door.

"So sorry, Mo," she would say. "But we just ain't ready for this pageant yet, so all distractions need to be gone during our practices."

I was, of course, saddened not to be able to spend the time with my friends. But more than that, I had caught Lynn staring at me several times when she thought I wasn't looking. In light of that, I would have liked to watch all of the rehearsals, if only to spend extra moments gawking back at the beautiful girl who had so bravely stood up to Nurse Wimble.

In the absence of my regular cohorts, I spent the better part of those final few visits getting better acquainted with the children who, like me, were not participating in the pageant for one reason or another. Timothy was one such child.

When I arrived at Timothy's room on the evening of December 22, I figured it would just be a short visit, but it ended up consuming the remainder of the night. The door was propped open, and he was sitting upright in bed, watching an animated Christmas special on television.

"Hi, Tim," I said. "Can I come in?"

"Sure! How is Santa's helper doing tonight?" he replied.

"Good, I guess."

Just then the commercial for the famed Air Jammer Road Rammer came on and we both began singing along with the theme song.

"Do you still want one of those for Christmas?" he asked excitedly when the commercial was over.

"Yeah, I suppose," I offered.

In truth, I hadn't really given it much thought since I'd started coming to visit the sick children at the hospital. I had been so absorbed in other things that I'd pretty much forgotten about what I wanted for Christmas. I had even forgotten about the grand gift Dr. Ringle had promised me for helping him out.

"Well, when you see Santa Claus again, tell him I still want one. I'd really like to see how fast it will go across the cafeteria floor!"

"You mean when I see Dr. Ringle again," I corrected.

"Yeah, Dr. Ringle—or Santa, it's the same thing. Molar, I told you before, Dr. Ringle *is* Santa Claus. Not just any old Santa Claus, he's the *real* Chris Kringle. I can feel it."

"Tim," I said guardedly, "For one thing, his name is Christoffer K. Ringle, not Chris Kringle. And I'm not even sure I believe in Santa Claus anymore. But if there is such a person, what proof do you have that Dr. Ringle is him? He doesn't exactly fit the bill, you know, with the wheelchair and being a doctor and all."

"It's him, I swear. I don't have any proof, but I bet we could get some if we looked hard enough. How about it?"

"You want to try to prove that he is Santa Claus? You mean snoop around and stuff? Spying on Dr. Ringle?"

"Well yeah, spying, if that's what you want to call it. We need to find out exactly where he goes every year, what he does there, and anything else we can find out. Maybe we can get into his office on the second floor and find clues."

"I dunno Tim, we could get into a lot of trouble."

Even as the words of caution coursed over my vocal chords and departed my mouth, I knew very well I was going to participate in Tim's proposed plan. I loved snooping—it was one of the things I considered myself good at. Getting into trouble, I figured, was just part of being a kid. I smiled at Tim.

"Then again," I continued, "it might be a lot of fun!"

"Cool!" he said as he jumped down from his bed. "You won't regret this. You'll see, he is Santa Claus!"

I doubted very much that anything would come of our investigation of Dr. Ringle, but it was at least a very exciting way to pass the time. Our first stop was the nurse's station, where Nurse Doyle was covering for Nurse Crowton who was helping Nurse Wimble at the pageant rehearsal.

"Hi there," she said kindly. "What can I do you for two fine gentlemen this evening?"

"Actually, we . . . um . . . need to, I mean, we need the combination for Dr. Ringle's locker downstairs in the doctor's changing area," I said sheepishly. "I'm one of his . . . ummm elves. He left some stuff there for me to give the kids, and he gave me his combination, but I lost it. Do you have it?" I hated lying, but I knew she'd never give us the combination if I told her what we were really up to.

"Is that so?" she asked skeptically.

"That's right," said Tim. "He's telling the truth. Totally."

Now Tim was lying too, but it seemed to work.

"Fine. I have his locker combination on file here," she said as she opened up a cabinet. "I wouldn't normally give it to you, but since he's out of town anyway, I'm sure it's empty. So have at it. But if anyone asks, don't mention my name. Okay?"

"Great!" I said as I took the combination from her.

Once we were downstairs we found Dr. Ringle's large locker right next to the two smaller ones he had reserved for Aaron and I on our first night at the hospital. I read the numbers in sequence to Timothy as he dialed in the code.

Click. The locker opened without complication. To our surprise, it was not empty at all as Nurse Doyle had supposed. Rather, it was stuffed full with hundreds, if not thousands, of letters addressed to 'Santa Claus, North Pole'. They all came tumbling out onto the floor as the door swung open.

"Would you look at that!" Timothy clamored. "I think we've found ourselves a clue. These are from all over the country. Why would letters to Santa come to Dr. Ringle if he was not, in fact, Santa Claus?"

"I dunno, Tim. I've got to admit, that's pretty weird. But it doesn't prove anything. Let's keep looking around and see if we can find any other clues."

Our second stop was to Dr. Ringle's office on the second floor. When we got there we found the door locked tight. Tim tugged and twisted on the handle several times in desperation, but it didn't budge.

"Hey you two's, what'd you's doing down there?"

We both turned around, startled that someone had caught us. A janitor, who had just stepped into the hallway from the bathroom he was cleaning, saw us loitering outside Dr. Ringle's office and was yelling as he approached.

"Uh, nothing," I lied for the second time that night. "We were just looking for a friend of ours."

"Oh yeah, you's doing nothing, huh? What'd I look like, a friggin idiot?" The janitor squatted down to look me directly in the eyes. For some reason he had a very familiar face.

"Do I know you?" I asked.

"Sorry kid," he said, ruffling my hair. "I can't say as how we've ever met. Now, you two's run along and stay out of trouble. I have to get back to my important sponsibilities." He pointed back to his cart of cleaning supplies.

Then it clicked. We *had* met before.

"You're the elf from the mall! You were handing out red papers at the end of the line—from New York, right?"

"That's right! You remember my ugly mug?"

"Your face? No, you look a lot different without the elf costume on. But I remember the funny way you talk."

He chuckled as he stood up. "So what'r you's doing here at the hospital? You ain't sick are ya?"

"Well I am," said Timothy cheerfully. "My name's Tim, and I got cancer. But this is Mo. He's an elf like you. He's been helping Santa Claus here at the hospital."

"Is that so Tim?" The janitor was smiling. He leaned down and patted Timothy on the arm. "I guess that makes each of us special, now, don't it? Two elves and the happiest patient I ever met—three special guys, without a doubt."

The janitor, who's name was Frank, told us he was working extra hours at the hospital to help pay the medical bills for his younger brother, who had been treated for cancer several months earlier. His brother was doing well now, but the bills were too much for his parents to cover on their own. So he had taken it upon himself to work at the hospital in his spare time, and all of his wages were given back to the hospital. It was while working there that he came to know Dr. Ringle and was given the opportunity to help out at the mall as an elf.

"Now tell me again," he said after he'd told us all about himself. "What you's two is doing here outside Dr. Ringle's office? And this time I want it straight, none o' this friggin nonsense about nothin' going on."

I looked at Tim before answering, and he nodded slightly,

encouraging me to let Frank in on our clandestine activities.

"The truth is we're looking for clues. We want to find out if Dr. Ringle is the one and only Santa Claus. Tim thinks he is, but I'm not even sure I believe in Santa Claus anymore."

"Well," said Frank knowingly. "I hate to admit it Mo, but Tim's right. Yup, I seen lots o' Saint Nick's in my day, but ain't none of them the real deal exceptin' for old Doc Ringle. And that's the truth. If you's wants, I'll let you in his office. Maybe there'll be somethin' there what proves who he is. How 'bout it?"

We gladly accepted the janitor's offer and were soon fumbling around through Dr. Ringle's stuff. Even though Frank had said so, I still wasn't entirely convinced that Dr. Ringle was Santa Claus. The thought crossed my mind that he might have just said those things to make Tim feel good on account of him having cancer.

"Look at this," cried Tim after a few minutes of searching.

Tim was holding up a brown paper bag.

"What's that, little man?"

"It says 'Reindeer Poop'!"

Sure enough, Tim opened up the bag and pulled out a handful of small brown pellets.

"Ooh," he moaned. "They're kinda squishy."

"What'd ya say, Mo? You wanted proof. Is that proof or what?" asked Frank with a grin.

"Deer poop! That's incredible," I said, trying hard to believe this might point to the existence of an actual Santa Claus.

Whatever the outcome of our investigation, I was unabashedly impressed with the poop. I'd never seen real deer poop before, and I could only think of one person in the world who would leave a bag of it lying around his office: Santa Claus.

"Good," he said. "Now you two's need to run along so's I can get back to work." He ruffled our hair again and herded us out the door. Tim carried the bag of poop along as evidence.

"Merry friggin' Christmas," Frank called jovially as we skipped off toward the elevators.

"Merry friggin' Christmas, Frank!" Tim yelled back as the elevator door opened.

"Yeah, thank's Frank," I added. "Merry Christmas!"

❖ ❖ ❖

Back on the fifth floor we exited the elevator and walked briskly back toward Tim's room where we hoped to further examine the reindeer droppings. On the way we passed by the nurse's station again. Nurse Doyle was no longer there, but Nurse Crowton was back from pageant rehearsal, and she looked eager to see us.

"Hi guys," she said as we approached. "Hold up Mo, I've got something for you."

"For me?"

"Yep, you and your elder elf brother," she quipped with a half-hearted smile.

"Oh," I replied. "Can it wait? We're sort of in a hurry?"

"Really?" she asked. "Just what have you two been up to while the rest of us have been at the Christmas pageant rehearsal?"

"Umm, well, we've sort of been. . . ."

"We've been trying to prove that Dr. Ringle is Santa Claus!" shouted Tim, unable to hide his enthusiasm. "And we've done it! We've found a bunch of clues! Well, a couple clues anyway. But we're pretty sure he's the one!" He was holding up the bag of poop.

"That's fantastic," said Nurse Crowton. "Maybe I can help add another clue. It just so happens that a letter came today from one Dr. Ringle, addressed to Mo and Aaron." She handed me the letter. "Why don't you read it?"

Tim was looking over my shoulder, trying to glean whatever he could from the envelope in my hand. "It's from the North Pole!" he shouted in my ear. "Look right there, it's postmarked from the North Pole! What other proof could you want?"

Tim was right. In red bold ink was a postmark, dated December 17, 1980, from the North Pole.

Just then Nurse Wimble meandered through two large swinging doors, and upon seeing that we were enjoying ourselves, immediately approached and asked what was wrong. Nurse Crowton explained in detail how we'd proven that Dr. Ringle is Santa Claus and showed her all of the clues we'd found. I could tell Nurse Crowton didn't fully buy into the whole Santa Claus thing, but she politely played along for our benefit.

Nurse Wimble wasn't so considerate.

"Nurse Crowton," she sneered, "I'm surprised you'd encourage these youngins' with such foolhardiness. I think they're old enough to know the truth, don't you?"

"Nurse Wimble, please don't. . . ." Nurse Crowton protested, but Nurse Wimble just ignored her.

"Now listen up y'all," she said. "You ain't found a single clue that proves Dr. Ringle is Santa Claus. And I'm gonna tell ya why. Those letters in his locker? They're the junk mail the post master doesn't know what to do with. Dr. Ringle likes to use them for some charity work he does. And the bag of feces you're holding?" Without so much as a second thought Nurse Wimble reached inside and grabbed a small handful of the brown squishy pellets, then tossed them in her mouth and began to chew.

My stomach lurched, and my gag reflex triggered almost simultaneously as she gnawed eagerly on the hardened pellets. In truth, it was probably Nurse Wimble's wicked laughter that ultimately pulled me back from the brink of vomiting. "Candy!" She jeered through a gloating brown smile. "Chocolate covered raisins. My favorite!" She was talking with her mouth full, and a small stream of juicy chocolate ran past her southern lips and down her chin. "And as for that there letter, why don't y'all take a closer look at the postmark?"

The envelope was still in my hand, so I held it up to examine it once more. My heart sank as I read the fine print. Not only was I disappointed to know the truth, but I was even sadder for Timothy, who had been so completely certain about the existence of areal Santa Claus in Dr. Christopher K. Ringle.

"Tim," I said slowly, hoping to let him down easy. "It's from Alaska. North Pole . . . Alaska."

Timothy leaned over and frowned when he read it for himself.

Nurse Wimble was gloating more than ever, almost gleeful that she should dash a young boy's hopes and dreams. "That's right, Alaska," she said flatly. "Dr. Ringle goes there every year. It's near a small Army Base outside of Fairbanks. They do a lot of work with the local children there this time of year. And to think, y'all thought there was a real North Pole! Sad, really, what they try to get children to believe these days."

"That's quite enough, Miss Wimble," said Nurse Crowton crossly. "Boys, why don't you head off and play and forget all about this silly conversation. You go on and believe whatever you like." She tried to force a smile, but it didn't really help. The damage had been done.

When we got back to Tim's room we agreed not to talk about Dr. Ringle anymore, or at least not about him being Santa Claus. Instead we found other important things to talk about. He told me all about his family; about how his parents came to visit him every morning and evening at the hospital; about how his older sister was the best speller in their whole school; and about the trip they took last year to Yellowstone Park. I told him about my mom and dad, about our home in Sherwood, and how I loved to play soccer and baseball.

Tim liked baseball, too but hadn't been able to play much recently because he had been in and out of the hospital so often. Since we didn't have a baseball to toss around, I found a pair of socks in Tim's dresser drawer and rolled them up tightly in a ball. For the rest of the evening we just sat playing catch across the room with socks.

It was a wonderful visit.

On the car ride home Aaron told me all about the latest and

greatest bloopers from their final dress rehearsal of the Christmas Pageant. Madhu, of course, continued to be a thorn in Nurse Wimble's side, especially since he hadn't yet decided what the fourth wise man should bring to give the Christ child. He kept promising her he would come up with something 'splendid indeed' but so far had come up with exactly nothing.

After he'd filled me in on everything noteworthy I told him about my visit with Timothy and the letter we'd received from Dr. Ringle. Mom turned on the overhead light in the car so we could read the letter together.

Dear Aaron & Mo,

I've heard some wonderful things about how you are helping at the hospital. I hope you know how much it means to the children to have visitors like you who spend time with them.

Mo, I was saddened to learn about your accident on the eighth floor. I trust you are recovering well by now. Please be more cautious next time you go for a ride on a gurney. Remember, those contraptions are designed to help the injured, not to injure the helpers!

I have had a wonderful visit at the Children's Center in Alaska. I began volunteering up here when I was in the Air Force and have continued the tradition ever since. There is a great need here for medical services, especially for children.

I will be returning to Oregon on Christmas Eve and should arrive at the hospital in time to watch the Christmas Pageant. Following the performance I shall once again require your elf assistance in handing out Christmas presents to the children.

Thank you again for all of your help. You have truly earned a gift worthy of this special season. See you soon!

Sincerely,

Dr. Christoffer K. Ringle, MD

CHAPTER

Ten

"Christmas Eve was a night of song that wrapped itself about you like a shawl. But it warmed more than your body. It warmed your heart . . . filled it, too, with melody that would last forever."

❁ Bess Streeter Aldrich ❁

The much-anticipated Christmas Pageant was held in the hospital's large cafeteria located on the second floor. It had been converted for the occasion into a fully operational auditorium, complete with stage, spotlights, and curtains. When my family and I entered the cafeteria, Nurse Wimble and her stage hands were scrambling around making last minute preparations for the big show. Madhu and his parents waved hello and invited us to sit with them in a few vacant seats near the front of the room.

"Have you decided what the fourth wise man will bring to baby Jesus?" I asked Madhu once I'd sat down.

"Oh dear, no. I am still very much undecided on that point," he said in his rhythmic Indian accent to which we'd all grown so accustomed. "But I have some good ideas, and Nurse Wimble has provided me with a fancy box. Now I must decide what to say is in the box when I set it down next to Jesus."

At the mention of her name, Nurse Wimble's ears perked up,

and she caught the tail end of what Madhu's was saying. Without missing a beat she marched over to give him one final piece of directorial guidance. "Mr. Amburi, you should have made a decision about this long before now! But since you haven't, I'll just make that decision for you. After the three *official* Wise Men have announced their special gifts, you are to set down the box beside the manger and say, 'I present you Lord, with a gift of precious gems—diamonds, pearls, and rubies—brought to you from my home far in the east.' Then you are done. Step back without making a scene, and we can all forget about the supposed fourth wise man. Do you understand me, Madhukar?"

She was not in a mood for lengthy intelligent responses, and Madhu knew better than to rebuff her in front of his parents. "Yes, Nurse Wimble, I understand," he replied politely.

"Good," she said flatly, then turned and walked away, returning all of her attention once more to the pre-show preparations.

"Well, she seems nice," joked my dad.

"Yes, well, nice or not, it's six forty-five," warned my mother. "Aaron, you and Madhu had better go get into your costumes. The pageant is supposed to start in fifteen minutes."

The two older boys made their way up to the stage and then disappeared behind the curtain. For the next fifteen minutes I sat watching the people as they entered the cafeteria. Occasionally

I spotted a boy or girl whom I'd met over the previous weeks and waved to them as best as I could with my one good arm. Many of them headed off to get into costume behind the stage, and it was in those few minutes that I finally felt the pangs of regret for having injured myself. Oh how I would have loved to participate in the Christmas Pageant but was instead sentenced to watch it from the sidelines.

The lights of the make-shift auditorium dimmed precisely at seven o'clock, indicating the performance was about to begin. Nurse Wimble took her seat in the front row when everything seemed in order and gave the cue for the lights to go down even further. From what I'd watched of the rehearsals, I knew that Aaron, as the narrator, was supposed to come on stage first, dressed up as a clergyman, to start things off.

He didn't come.

The audience sat quietly for a few minutes, but soon whispers and questions began to erupt throughout the hall. All the while a lone spotlight swept back and forth across the stage in search of my brother. Eventually, and none too soon, the curtain parted and Aaron stepped into view. But rather than walk over to the side of the stage where a microphone was waiting for him, he strutted straight down the stage stairs and rushed over to Nurse Wimble.

I couldn't hear what he was whispering to her, but by the look on his face it was something very important. Nurse Wimble, on the other hand, appeared as though it was just another trivial annoyance. Out of apparent obligation she stood up, turned around, and marched unenthusiastically over to where I was sitting with my parents.

"Molar," she said softly as she leaned down. "You are friends with Miss Katrina Barlow, correct?"

"Yes mam," I said softly.

"Well, it appears she has come up missing. The other angels can't find her anywhere. As her friend, you may want to go look for her. But I will *not* delay this performance on her account! If you can find her before her scene begins, fine. Otherwise, I'm sure the angels will do quite alright without her and her paper bag."

"Thank you, mam," I said. I wasn't really sure what I was thanking her for but thought it sounded nice anyway.

With my parents consent I slid out of the row of chairs and fumbled my way through the darkness up the aisle toward the green-glowing exit sign at the rear. As the door closed behind me I could just hear my brother beginning his lines, signaling the Christmas Pageant was under way.

CHAPTER

Eleven

"It is not known precisely where angels dwell—whether in the air, the void, or the planets. It has not been God's pleasure that we should be informed of their abode."

❁ Voltaire ❁

I *don't have much time*, I thought as I hurried toward the elevators at the other end of the building. After making my way up to the fifth floor, I walked down the corridor that led to Katrina's room. Since everyone was supposed to be downstairs watching the pageant, the staff had dimmed the lights lower than normal, which made me feel all the more alone as I paced along the empty hallway.

As I got closer to the doorway near the end of the corridor, I noticed a flickering of red and green lights pulsating through the darkness. Katrina's door was partially open, allowing the flashing colors to escape.

"Katrina?" I whispered as I touched the door lightly, pushing it open all the way. "Katrina, are you in there?"

Within the room I saw the source of the red and green lights. Dr. Ringle, in his full Santa Claus costume, was seated in his wheelchair, his famed 'sleigh' twinkling in the darkness. His back was towards me as he sat looking out at the rain pouring down against the window.

"She's not here lad," he said as he began to turn his wheels slowly around. "I've looked everywhere. I'm afraid she doesn't want to be found."

"But she's gonna miss her part in the pageant! She's part of the angel choir, and after all her practicing and singing she should be there."

"I'm sorry, Mo. You've been such a good friend to her. I know it means a lot to you to see her in the pageant—it's what you broke your arm for. But unless we find her there's nothing we can do."

"That's it!" I shouted.

"What's it?" he said, looking downright puzzled.

"My arm! I know where Katrina is! Follow me!"

With Dr. Ringle jingling along in hot pursuit, I ran back down the corridor and made my way to the service elevator in the east corner of the building. Once we were both inside I pushed the top button to floor number eight.

When the elevator stopped and the doors parted, I found myself back where I'd been on the night of my accident, looking down a gently sloping hallway towards a stairwell. There, sitting on the top step with her paper-bag head resting on her shoulder, was Katrina. She was dressed all in white with the feathery form of wings protruding from her back. Dr. Ringle and I approached slowly.

"You look like a beautiful angel," I said once I was close enough to talk without yelling. She didn't respond or even move for that matter. "How come you're up here when the pageant is going on downstairs?"

Still no response.

"Kat, Dr. Ringle is back from up north. He's here, too."

With that she lifted her head and turned around slowly to look at him through the holes in her white bag, which was now showing considerable signs of wear.

"Hi Santa," she said. I could tell by her voice that she had been crying before our arrival.

"Hello, lass. I've missed you."

"I've missed you, too. I wanted to tell you thanks."

"For what, Miss Katrina?" Dr. Ringle was smiling broadly now.

"You know what," she stated matter-of-factly. "For my Christmas present—the one I wrote on that red paper."

"Oh yes! Well, you're quite welcome. But you earned it you know."

"You mean you already gave her a Christmas present?" I asked.

Now I was the one with the puzzled look on my face. I didn't understand how Dr. Ringle could possibly have given her a

Christmas present considering he had been gone for so long and was just seeing Katrina again for the first time in weeks.

"In a manner of speaking, lad. In a manner of speaking. But Christmas presents are not important right now. Right now we should be talking about getting one Katrina Barlow back down to the Christmas Pageant. I hear word they are missing one of their most special angels."

"I'm not going. I can't."

"But why, Katrina? You've done so well in rehearsals!" I pleaded.

She turned and finally looked right at me with those big green eyes. "Mo, it was different at rehearsals. All of the kids are used to seeing the weirdo with the bag on her head. But there are a lot of people in the audience who will laugh at me if I go out there. They'll think it's some sort of joke. I don't want them laughing, not at me. I just want to be left alone, where nobody will laugh."

"They won't laugh," I said sympathetically. But I knew better. People always laugh when they don't understand.

"They will, and you know it. I can't go out on stage without the bag cuz' I'm ugly—and that'd scare 'em half to death. And I can't go with it because they'll laugh at me."

"You are not ugly," I said.

"How do you know? You've never even seen me."

"I did see you, once. After we crashed at the bottom of those stairs, I saw you. Your bag must've come off when we were falling. Right before I passed out I saw you standing over me. You're not ugly, Katrina."

Katrina lifted her head and turned to look me right in the eyes, searching as if to see whether or not I was telling the truth.

"You're just a beautiful girl who has a sickness," I continued. "That's all. Besides, the way I see it, your beauty goes a whole lot deeper than most people's, so what they think or say about you doesn't really matter, does it?"

She was quiet, but her eyes showed she was trying to assess the value of what I'd just said.

"But . . ." she said finally, trying hard to mask the fact that she was getting a bit choked up. "So what? Just because you don't think I'm ugly doesn't make it so. I'm not going on stage without the bag. And I'm not going with it either. I'll just sit here until it's all over. Besides, I've had an awful headache for a couple days, and I don't feel up to it."

I could tell Dr. Ringle was concerned when she mentioned the headache, but he didn't say anything about it so we all sat silently again for several moments longer.

"Kat," I said eventually. "Would you go on stage if you weren't the only one wearing a bag?"

"What do you mean?"

"Just what I said. Would you go down and be in the pageant if you were not the only one with a bag on your head?"

"I . . . I suppose. Why?"

"Great!" I said. "Dr. Ringle, will you please take Katrina down to the Christmas Pageant? I'll meet you backstage in five minutes!"

"But Mo!" Katrina shouted as I ran off at a full sprint. "Wait! Mo! What are you doing?"

I didn't have time to respond. If Katrina was going to make it on stage in time for her part, then I didn't have a single moment to lose.

CHAPTER

Twelve

"The only gift is a portion of thyself."

❁ Ralph Waldo Emerson ❁

Shepherds and sheep were lining up at the side of the stage by the time I finally slipped through the back door of the cafeteria, which meant the angel scene was not far off. I didn't see Katrina or Dr. Ringle, but I found the flock of angels loitering around a large plate of Christmas cookies and punch while they waited for their grand entrance on stage. I hurried over to join them.

"Hi guys," I said, catching my breath.

"Hello," said a curly haired girl whom I recognized as having hurt Katrina's feelings on at least one prior occasion. "You're the bag girl's friend, right? Have you found her?"

"Don't call her that!" I snapped. "How would you like it if people called you things like that? She has a name. It's Katrina."

"Sorry," she replied and seemed to mean it. "That wasn't very nice, I know. Have you found Katrina? We were all really worried about her . . . *really.*"

"Yes, I found her," I said. "But she's a little nervous about going out on stage. She's embarrassed, and I need your help to fix that."

In as few words as I could but with the speed of Madhu himself, I explained to the angel chorus all about Katrina, about her sickness, about her mother, about the recent loss of her grandfather, and about how hard it is when people make fun and call her things like 'the bag girl.' I told them everything I could think of. Then I showed them a stack of paper Christmas bags I had found all throughout the hospital and asked them if they would be willing to wear a bag like Katrina when they went on stage so she wouldn't stand out in the crowd.

To my utter amazement, and as proof that miracles have not ceased, every one of those children agreed to my plan without hesitation.

With great haste, we cut out eye and mouth holes in the bags. I helped some of the younger angels while the older kids did their own. Even the curly haired girl seemed genuinely happy to be putting on a bag. I was just slipping the last paper bag over a little boy's head when I heard someone speak my name.

"Mo?" It was Katrina.

I turned around to face her. She was standing next to Dr. Ringle, who was sitting motionless in his blinking wheelchair. True to my own naivety, I had no idea why there were large tears rolling down his rosy cheeks.

"What are you doing?" she asked.

"Nothing . . . I . . . I just." I fumbled over my words, not quite sure what I should say. "You said if you weren't the only one on stage with a bag that you'd go out there. Well? What do you think?"

She didn't say anything. I half expected her to turn tail and run away. I was only half right. She ran, but instead of making for the nearest exit, she darted straight towards me, nearly knocking me to the floor as she draped her arms around my neck and gave me a hug.

The moment, however, was to be short lived.

"I think we missed our cue!" shouted one of the taller angels. I couldn't tell which one amid all of the paper covered faces.

All of the angels fell instantly quiet as we listened to Aaron's voice piping through the sound system.

"And I repeat!" he boomed into the microphone, loud enough to cause static feedback in the speakers. "Suddenly there was a multitude of the heavenly host praising God and saying 'Glory to God in the highest, and on earth peace, good will toward men!' And then . . . the angels came!" Aaron was stalling—hoping and pleading that the flying host of heaven would appear.

"Let's go!" said Katrina, leading the way. Then she stopped

abruptly and looked back at me. "Mo, come with us. There's one more bag over there."

All of the angels were waiting behind Katrina while the narrator's voice continued to stall in the background, now sounding ever more frantic.

"If any of us is an angel, it's *you,*" she begged.

I didn't know what to say. Sure, I'd been told under no uncertain terms that I couldn't participate, but I wanted to be part of the pageant *so* bad.

"Fine," I said with sarcastic reluctance. "But if anyone asks, it was you who twisted my arm!"

"What's new?" she giggled. "I was the one who broke it to begin with."

Slipping the bag over my head I rushed up to the front of the line to join Katrina, and then we all flew onto the stage. The music started as soon as we were in sight, and all of the angels began singing as we took our place in the center of the stage. I didn't know the words, so I just mouthed and hummed along.

When Nurse Wimble saw us she nearly jumped right up to high heaven. There were a few whispers and chuckles from the audience as everyone tried to decipher why this flock of tardy angels had bags on their heads, and why the angel near the front with a cast on his arm had no wings and was wearing a red flannel shirt and jeans. I glanced only briefly at Nurse Wimble as we all shuffled into place, but that was long enough to tell she would have more than a few biblical expressions to say to us all later.

After a few rousing Christmas carols including *Angels We Have Heard on High, Hark! The Herald Angels Sing,* and *Joy to the World,* the angels moved to a spot near the side of the stage so the final scene could proceed.

I sat watching intently as Mary held her newborn baby and sang a song I'd never heard before called *Mary's Lullaby*. It was a beautiful tune, sung by none other than Lynn, the feisty young woman who had threatened to quit the pageant unless Katrina be allowed to participate. Her voice was a melody that rang clear and true when she sang, and I understood at once why Nurse Wimble had been so quick to give in to her demands.

When her song was finished, the fabled shepherds came to see the infant, and everyone on stage joined them in singing *Away In A Manger.* During that song Katrina reached up and grabbed hold of my arm. I think she was crying when the words of one verse said, 'Bless all the dear children in Thy tender care, and fit us for Heaven to live with Thee there.' And I'm not one hundred percent sure, but I might have been crying then too as I thought about Katrina and some of the other children at the hospital who would probably see heaven long before me.

One of the final songs of the Christmas Pageant was *We Three Kings*. I couldn't help but laugh when I saw the lanky fourth wise man rumble onto the stage, his gold and purple crown hanging slightly askew on his narrow head, and his wide grin beaming from ear to ear. The song was about three wise men, not four, which is probably why Nurse Wimble had been so opposed to adding Madhu in the first place. At the end of the song, the Wise Men each presented their gifts as they bowed before Joseph, Mary, and the new Christ child.

The tallest of the Wise Men, who carried a leather pouch, was the first of the bunch to speak. "The gift I bring is gold—truly a gift fit for a King."

Then the second wise man stepped forward and bowed. "I, too, bring a gift worthy of the Lord. Frankincense, from my home in the east." Stepping back, he made room for the third wise man to approach the manger.

"I come from afar to see the Messiah. I bring him myrrh, the most precious gift of my country." That particular wise man was played by a girl, but it didn't seem to matter.

When it was Madhu's turn to step forward and present his gift, for some reason he didn't do anything at all. He just stood frozen in place holding the wooden box, his eyes riveted on the baby lying in the manger. The third wise man backed up a few paces and elbowed him in the ribs. Madhu jerked a little bit and snapped back from wherever his mind had wandered, but instead of approaching the manger, he turned and faced the audience.

"I, too, come from the east," he said.

I had never heard Madhu speak so slowly. Every word came out clear and measured.

"I was born in India and do not know much of your religion. I do not know if this child is the Savior. But from what I have read he is certainly a great prophet. He will be worshipped by many as the very Son of God."

The auditorium was deathly silent as he spoke. From where I stood huddled with the angels I could see that Nurse Wimble was slouching in her seat, her hands completely covering her face, which was now flushed bright red.

"I have read from the Bible," he continued, "of the things he will do and the things he will teach when he gets older. Surely, this young child is destined for greatness and worthy of the world's greatest gifts. But," he paused, letting the word hang in the air for several seconds. "I have no such gift to bring him."

There was a collective gasp through the room as Madhu opened up an empty box. Then he began speaking again.

"One day, this child will tell those who follow him, '*If ye love me, keep my commandments*.' And what will he command them?

'This is my commandment, that ye love one another, as I have loved you.' If this is truly the Son of God, then there is no worldly gift that he needs. He does not ask for gold, or wealth, or money. He asks only that we love others. And so, that will be my gift to him. I will try harder to love everyone, regardless of who they are or what they look like." He turned slightly to the left and smiled directly at Katrina, then went on speaking. "And I will try to overlook the few things that make us all different and focus instead on the many things that make us the same."

A single tear dropped from the corner of Madhu's eye and trickled down his face. He turned back to the baby and set down his empty box, kneeling gracefully at the foot of the manger.

"It is a small gift, I know, but it is the only thing I have to offer Christ."

❊ ❊ ❊

Aaron stood at the front of the stage holding his script at his side, unsure of how best to continue following Madhu's impromptu sermon. No one in the audience spoke. Finally my brother inched closer to the microphone, his mind racing to find something—anything—to say.

"Uhh. . . ," he started. "And so we see that the Wise Men all brought different gifts to baby Jesus. And . . . some wise men were

. . . uhhmmm . . . wiser than others."

Just then I felt a tug on my arm. Katrina was taking a step forward and was pulling me with her.

"What are you doing?" I whispered from beneath my bag. She didn't say anything but just kept walking across the stage towards the manger with me in tow.

Aaron saw us walking and tried to fill in a narration as we went. "And then suddenly, two wayward angels stepped forward from heaven to visit the Christ Child."

The audience laughed hysterically at that, but Nurse Wimble had had quite enough. She shot up out of her chair and screamed, "What do you angels think you're doing? This is not what we practiced!"

"And God rebuked his angels and told them to return to heaven at once," said Aaron over the sound system.

Again, Nurse Wimble was not as amused as everyone else. She placed her hands firmly on her hips and gave my brother a look that warned of severe consequences unless he stopped talking immediately.

Katrina, however, was undeterred. As the audience settled down she quietly pulled me over to the manger. When she got there, she stood staring thoughtfully down at Jesus. Her green eyes were fixed on the doll lying in the hay, bound tightly in a hospital blanket. Then, without a word, she turned and pulled the mask from off my head. It was, admittedly, refreshing to have it gone, but I didn't understand why she had done it or what she was up to. Before I could puzzle it out on my own, she knelt down, and in the hushed silence that now gripped everyone watching, Katrina slowly lifted her trembling hands to her own head and peeled off the bag that had hidden her face for so many months.

With the spotlight shining on us both, there was no hiding the physical reality of Katrina's appearance from anyone in the great room. Most of her hair was gone, with patches of stubble scattered here and there across her otherwise bald scalp. The brain tumor and the associated treatments had left her skin withered and cracked, with open lesions visible just above her forehead and thick scars from multiple surgeries extending from the crown of her head to the nape of her neck. The shape of her head was abnormal, bulging on one side and sunken on the other. Sections of her misshapen scalp had been grafted together with not-quite-matching colors of skin to cover up the invasiveness of the operations she had endured. And perhaps most notable of all was a relatively new development: a large, lumpy swelling of tissue protruding from an area high above her left ear and ending down in the softness of her delicate cheek.

Nobody on the stage or in the audience made so much as a

whisper as Katrina carefully folded the white bag in at the corners, then over again in half to make it smaller, and placed it gently down at Jesus' feet. Turning back again to look up at me, still kneeling near the Christ child, she whispered so only I could hear, "It's all I have to give." Then she stood slowly, took me by the arm again and led me back to the choir.

In that flash of a moment I considered what it was that Katrina had just done. Had she given a simple paper bag to the 'Lord of Lords' and 'King of Kings'? No, I guessed it was probably much more than that. It might have been that the weathered paper bag was no less than the single most valuable possession she had, and therefore, an undeniably excellent gift for the Savior. Or perhaps she was offering the Christ her own pride, exposing the scars of her own self doubt at the feet of him who is mighty to heal. Whatever the case, I knew her sacrifice was more than I could fully appreciate, let alone articulate.

As we walked slowly away from the manger, a voice in the audience began to sing. It was a woman's voice with a familiar southern accent, and she was singing in a faint, choked voice.

"Silent night, Holy night, all is calm, all is bright."

I looked up to see Nurse Wimble, the bane of all patients and elves, standing in front of her chair, doing all she could to keep her composure as the words of the familiar tune broke free from her lips. Others soon joined in, standing one by one, and before we made it back to our spot everyone in the room was singing together.

As the song progressed, the angels each began to follow Katrina's lead, removing their paper bags, revealing the tears that stained their young faces.

When the song ended, the spotlight moved from away from Katrina to a red and green blinking wheelchair making it's way ever so slowly across the stage. Dr. Ringle, dressed as Santa, was headed for the microphone. Aaron was eager to hand it to him.

"I've heard it said that the true meaning of Christmas has been forgotten, that the Christmas spirit is dead." Dr. Ringle's deep Scottish voice echoed through the hall. "I think our Christmas Pageant this evening would suggest otherwise." He reached up and removed the red and white hat from his head and rested it in his lap. "With that in mind, I would like to announce a slight change to our proceedings. Due to the fact that it would spoil an otherwise perfect evening, Santa Claus will not be handing out presents to the children here at this event. Instead, gifts will be delivered to each room individually later this evening. Thank you all for joining us here tonight. Merry Christmas, and God Bless you all."

For some time afterward people just milled around the cafeteria wishing each other a Merry Christmas and congratulating one another for a great performance. I got the sense that no one really wanted to leave, that they somehow hoped the pageant and the feelings they felt would continue on indefinitely.

Everyone, including grumpy Nurse Wimble, felt something special that night, something magical. Only it wasn't magic at all but the true spirit of Christmas, and it left us all with a desire to be better people, to be more giving and forgiving, and to reach out to those around us in all their unique and varied circumstances.

But all good things must come to an end, and eventually we had to go home. Aaron and I said goodbye to as many children as we could, wishing them all a very Merry Christmas and Happy New Year. Even though our time volunteering at the hospital was officially over, we hoped to return again soon to visit all of our new friends.

Katrina was especially sad to see us go, but she gave us both a big hug and wished us well.

"Mo," she said as we were leaving. "Thank you."

I smiled, nodded, and then we went home to be together as a family for Christmas.

CHAPTER

Thirteen

"Somehow, not only for Christmas but all the long year through, the joy that you give to others is the joy that comes back to you. And the more you spend in blessing the poor and lonely and sad, the more of your heart's possessing returns to you glad."

❁ John Greenleaf Whittier ❁

It was barely seven o'clock in the morning on Christmas day when we heard the sirens blaring outside our house. Dad and Mom were still making breakfast in their pajamas, and none of the presents under the tree had been opened yet.

I peeked out through the kitchen window and saw Dr. Ringle waving frantically from the passenger seat of an orange and white ambulance.

"Dr. Ringle is here!" I shouted. "Hurry up, he wants something!"

When we got outside, Dr. Ringle explained that during the night Katrina's condition had taken a drastic turn for the worse. "The headaches she had been complaining about for the past few days were because of pressure inside her skull," he said. "The tumor has been growing rapidly over the last week, and it is now squeezing everything else out. We knew it would come to this eventually," he continued gravely. "We just didn't know when.

She wants to see Mo, but I'm afraid there isn't much time."

Four weeks earlier I might have needed a little help understanding what he meant when he said there isn't much time. But I had grown up a lot in those weeks, and now I understood perfectly well.

Katrina was going to die soon.

Dad and Mom agreed to let me go with Dr. Ringle in the ambulance back to the hospital. The rest of the family would change out of their pajamas and then drive over as quickly as they could in the station wagon.

With sirens roaring and lights spinning we made our way to the hospital in record time. It helped that there were very few cars and pedestrians out and about because of the holiday, which made it infinitely easier to plow through intersections and red lights without touching the brake pedal.

When we arrived at the hospital, the ambulance driver helped Dr. Ringle into his wheelchair, and then we raced inside the emergency entrance and up to the fifth floor. I slowed as I approached Katrina's room. There, tacked to her door just below her nameplate, was the crayon-drawn sign: *E.D. 12/79*. I didn't have an obvious reason to, but something compelled me to reach up and take it down. I pulled out the tack that held it in place and then followed Dr. Ringle into Katrina's room.

Inside, a nurse was busy adjusting a monitor near the bed.

Katrina was wired to an electronic device that blinked repeatedly with each new heartbeat. She was also hooked up to an I.V. through a large needle in her arm. It was obvious she was in a great deal of pain, but her eyes lit up when she saw me.

"You made it," she said weakly; her mouth forming a faint smile.

"Of course—wouldn't want to be anywhere else. Merry Christmas." I didn't know what else to say. Then I remembered the paper in my hand that I'd just removed from her door, and I held it out to her. "Look," I said. "You beat the doctors by a whole year!" She tried to laugh, but it hurt too much. Instead of laughing she winced in pain.

"Mo, I wanted you to come so I could say thank you."

"For last night? Oh, it was nothin'."

"Not for last night. For everything. For helping Santa with my Christmas gift. It was pretty much the best gift ever."

As usual, I was a little confused. I hadn't helped Dr. Ringle at all with her gift. I had not even gotten the red Christmas list from her like I'd been told.

"But Kat," I exclaimed honestly. "I didn't help him. Whatever he gave you for Christmas he did on his own."

"Yes, you did," she whispered, her voice growing more shallow with every breath. "And now I'd like to give you something for

Christmas. I know it's not much, but hopefully it will help you remember."

She reached down over the side of the bed, straining to keep her head from moving too much, and pulled up a wooden box with a bow on top. I recognized the box as the one Madhu had carried the night before in the Christmas Pageant.

"Open it," she said softly as she lifted it across the bed and placed it in my hands.

Tears began to fall freely from my eyes before I even touched the lid. With my lips trembling and fingers shaking I lifted it open slowly to find a white, worn out paper bag, neatly folded up. Beside the bag was a red piece of paper all crumpled up in a ball.

I pulled the bag from the box first and unfolded it. There, as I'd seen so many times, were the three familiar holes—two for the eyes, one for the mouth.

Next I grabbed the red paper ball. It was the list I was supposed to collect from Katrina on my second visit to the hospital, the same one she swore was only for Santa to read. She had also been sure that even Santa, no matter how magical he was, would never be able to give her what she wanted for Christmas. With surgical precision I unraveled the red paper. The back of the page, which was now heavily wrinkled, was full of familiar blank lines—the same lines I had once tried desperately to fill with just about every toy known to man. Flipping the ragged paper over I read anew the title, printed in bold typed letters across the top: "All I Want For Christmas Is. . . ." I struggled then as I wiped away the tears, to read the simple words that Katrina had written on the first line of the paper: *A Friend.*

"Thank you Kat," I said as I rubbed my eyes on my coat sleeve. "That's the best Christmas gift I've ever gotten." When I looked up at Katrina, she was smiling ever so slightly. Her eyes were closed, and she looked peaceful, happier than I'd ever seen her. "Kat?" When she didn't reply I lifted my head just enough to observe that the monitor next to her bed had stopped blinking.

"She's gone, lad," said Doctor Ringle as he wheeled over and clasped my shoulder.

"I know," I said. I was sad Katrina was gone but happy her pain was over and that she could be with her mom and grandfather again.

As I sat looking at her, a Christmas song stirred somewhere in my mind, and soon I was humming along as I remembered the words to one of the verses: '*Bless all the dear children in Thy tender care, and fit us for Heaven to live with Thee there.*'

CHAPTER

Fourteen

"Silently, one by one, in the infinite meadows of heaven,
blossomed the lovely stars, the forget-me-nots
of the angels."

❁ Henry Wadsworth Longfellow ❁

"What'a you's doing here on Christmas little man?" asked Frank, the janitor-elf from the Bronx, as I sat down next to him in the hospital's main lobby.

"Just waiting," I said. "Dr. Ringle asked me to stay here until my parents arrive. A friend of mine passed away today. I came to say goodbye."

"You ain't talking 'bout Kat-B on floor five, are ya?"

"Katrina Barlow, yes, that's her. Do you know her?"

"My kid brother introduced me to her when he was here. Since then I haven't seen much of her, ya know, but I've tried to say hi and what not when I'm up there cleaning the bat'rooms. Then this mornin' I get's a call from Doc Ringle, says he want's to meet me here. Said it had somethin' to do with Kat-B. So I guess we're here for da same thing."

I enjoyed talking to Frank very much—he was kind and thoughtful, even if he talked funny—but our conversation was cut short when my family rushed through the hospital's front doors with Aaron in tow.

"Mo?" said my mom when she saw me. "Is everything alright?"

"Yep. Everything is fine," I said solemnly as I cradled the wooden box on my lap. "She . . . she passed away about twenty minutes ago."

Mom and Dad were glad to see I was taking it so well, but they were understandably sad for the loss of my friend. "Dr. Ringle wants us all to go upstairs," I continued. "Says he has a surprise for everyone."

"Mind if I join you's," asked Frank. "Doc wanted me up there in a few minutes anyway—said somethin' 'bout a special Christmas gift."

My family and Frank followed me back up to the fifth floor where Dr. Ringle was waiting in his wheelchair near the nurse's station. Madhu's parents were also waiting there.

"Oh, I'm so glad you're all here. Now we can get started," declared Dr. Ringle.

"Started with what?" asked Aaron

"With what? Why, with the presents, lad. It is Christmas, after all! And what better way to celebrate Christ's birth than to give gifts, just as the *four* Wise Men did so long ago!"

"But I thought the presents were gonna be given out last night?" I said.

"Aye, most of them were delivered last night, of course, by 'Ole Saint Nicholas himself. But there are a few very special gifts remaining for some very special people. Now come along, follow me."

Dr. Ringle's smile was never bigger than when he led all of us —me, Aaron, Mom and Dad, Frank, and Madhu's parents—down the hallway to Madhu's room.

"Ho, ho, ho! Merry Christmas," bellowed Dr. Ringle as he pushed open the door without knocking. "And how are you on this fine morning?"

"Oh, very well," said Madhu without hesitation. "Yes, I'm definitely doing quite fine. But I am wondering why all of you are here?"

"Well," responded Dr. Ringle, "we're here to deliver a little Christmas joy. You do want your Christmas gift, don't you?"

"Oh," Madhu said, blushing a little. "I assumed I was not getting one when you didn't come last night. I saw you going to all the other rooms."

"Ah, I see," sighed Dr. Ringle. "And did you think that perhaps you wouldn't get a present because you ripped up your Christmas list and threw it in the garbage?"

Madhu blinked hard. "How did you know I threw it in the garbage?" He looked over at Aaron and I, but we didn't know either.

"Just answer the question, lad," said the doctor.

Madhu nodded and quietly said, "Yes sir."

"And did you rip up the list because you thought Santa wouldn't bring you a gift on account of your religion?" asked Dr. Ringle. His eyes twinkled with kindness as he spoke.

Madhu nodded again.

"Madhukar, I apologize that your present was delayed, but I do have a very special gift for the wisest among wise men. It's from Santa and one of his very special friends."

With that, Dr. Ringle reached deep into the burgundy colored velvet sack that hung from the back of his wheelchair and pulled out a red piece of paper. To be more precise, it was lots of small pieces of paper, all taped together to form one complete puzzle.

"My list!" shouted Madhu. "How did you get it?"

"Ho, ho, ho! Just a little Christmas magic," hollered Dr. Ringle.

Everyone gathered around to see what Madhu had written on his Christmas list. It was difficult to decipher through all of the broken edges of paper. Madhu's father was the first to sound it out.

"All I want for Christmas is . . . A new liver, so I can go home with my family," he said.

Madhu's mother sobbed when she heard the words.

"Dr. Ringle, you should not joke about such things," she cried. "It is cruel to raise a boy's hopes over a gift you cannot give."

"Mrs. Amburi, there is something else you should hear as well." Dr. Ringle reached again into his bag and pulled out another piece of paper, this one white and folded up neatly. "Here Madhu, it' addressed to you. Would you read it aloud?"

Madhu took the note from the doctor and unfolded it carefully. On the top of the page was a crayon-drawn picture, a self-portrait of sorts, of a young girl with beautiful long brown hair and bright green eyes. She had wings like an angel and seemed to be singing.

Madhu cleared his throat and began reading slowly.

"Dear Mad-who, How are you? I'm fine. But the doctors say I'm not. It's late at night on Christmas Eve, and they have hooked me up to lots of things. Dr. Ringle says that probably by tomorrow I will be going home for good to be with my family. I found your Christmas list in the garbage and taped it back together so I could give it to Santa Claus for you. Dr. Ringle say's he's not Santa, but I know he is because he gave me just what I wanted for Christmas. Thank you for being a friend to me, along with Mo and Aaron. I have been so happy! I want you to be happy, too. Since I'm going home to my family, you should be able to go home to your family, too. So I have told the doctors that you may have my liver. I won't need it anymore. I hope it works well for you. I never had any problems with it. With Love, Katrina Barlow."

Dr. Ringle tried to speak above the bittersweet sobs in the room, especially those of Madhu's parents. "We just got the results back from the lab, and it looks like her liver will be a good match for you. Thanks to Katrina we've found a viable donor for your transplant! But timing on this is very important, so I've already scheduled the procedure for this afternoon. I know it's probably not what you had planned for this holiday, lad, but the upside is that you'll be recovering at home by New Year's day."

Everyone was amazed at Katrina's generosity and at Dr. Ringle's persistent dedication to helping the children. This was a magical man if ever there was one. We all gave Madhu a big hug, and then Dr. Ringle asked for our attention one last time.

"Well, there is just one final thing I wish to discuss," he said, focusing his gaze on Aaron and I, who were sitting in the chairs next to Madhu's bed. "I promised two young elves that if they helped me at the hospital they would receive a gift far better than anything they had ever wanted. Does anyone remember that?"

Aaron and I both nodded hesitantly. Neither of us wanted to take away from Madhu's excitement just then. Nor did we want a reward for visiting the children.

"Dr. Ringle," said Aaron, speaking for both of us. "You don't have to give us anything. We don't need any more toys. It's been more than we expected just being able to help out around here. Plus, we both made great friends, so what more could we want?"

"Aye," said Dr. Ringle softly. "What more indeed? The fact is, you've already received everything I hoped you would. There's nothing left for me to give you more than you have already found on your own through service and friendship. Well done, lads. Well done."

Dr. Ringle gave us all a final hug and then extracted his Santa costume from his bag. He pulled the coat over his arms and shoulders, placed the red and white hat on top of his head, and then wheeled around to the doorway.

"I'm heading up north again for a while but will probably check in on you from time to time," he said as he rolled through the doorway. "Ho, ho . . . oh no! Frank, how could I forget? I've still got one tiny little matter of business." Dr. Ringle rolled his blinking sleigh back into the room and right up next to Frank, who was standing stiff against the near wall. "This, my good man, is for you, janitor extra ordinaire, compliments of Katrina and the other persons responsible for handling the Barlow trust." Dr. Ringle handed him a sealed envelope. "She said you deserved it for all of your hard work on your brother's behalf and for simply smiling at her when no one else would."

Frank took the envelope and opened it. Within a matter of seconds he had to stop reading to wipe the tears from his face.

"Yo, ho, ho, Doc Ringle! Merry friggin' Christmas!" he shouted in disbelief. "Is this for real?"

Enclosed in the envelope was the outstanding medical bill for Frank's younger brother. The balance due was zero. Katrina's trust fund had paid it all in full.

"Real indeed," replied Dr. Ringle. "Merry Christmas. And God Bless you all!"

Dr. Ringle wheeled around once more and made for the hallway. As he tugged the door closed behind him, I remembered something Katrina had written in her letter to Madhu—about her believing that Dr. Ringle was Santa Claus. Timothy, down the hall, had said the same thing on several occasions.

"Dr. Ringle, wait!" I yelled as I jumped up and ran to the door. "Why do so many people say you are the real Santa."

I yanked the door open as fast as I could, not a moment after it clicked shut, but there was no one there. The hallway was completely empty. It was impossible he could have gotten away so fast, yet the only person in the hallway was me.

Dr. Christoffer K. Ringle was inexplicably, unfathomably, undeniably gone in the twinkling of an eye.

Timothy opened his door and stepped into the hallway.

"Looking for someone?" he asked with a knowing grin.

"Dr. Ringle was right here. Where'd he go? Did you hear him come by your room?"

"Not exactly. Christmas magic is silent, Mo. You don't hear it; you feel it; you know it; you believe it. I believe it, regardless of what old Nurse Wimble said. Dr. Ringle *is* Santa Claus."

"Maybe you're right," I admitted as I thought about all of the Christmas miracles I'd witnessed in the last twenty-four hours.

Aaron stepped into the hallway and put his arm around my shoulder. "Maybe you were right about something too, Mo. I think Santa was a wise guy after all."

"Mo, I got a new pair of socks for Christmas," said Tim. "Want to play catch in my room for a while?"

"That sounds great," I said.

And it was.

Epilogue

I've never really understood who 'they' are, but they say time flies when you're having fun. If they are correct, then the years since 1980 must have been one long drawn-out party because in the twinkling of an eye, I'm all grown up with a wife and children of my own. Christmases have come and gone since then, each one a special reminder of life's greatest gifts, but none has been more memorable than my first *real* Christmas all those years ago.

Last Thursday was Thanksgiving, which was a wonderful time with family, but the following day was even better.

I woke up early and pulled out all of the Christmas decorations, making sure to not break any of the fragile pieces of my wife's collection of Nativity scenes (Lynn has been accumulating the beautiful crèche's since she was a patient in the Children's Hospital years ago). Then I loaded all of our Christmas music onto the computer and let the gentle sounds of Bing Crosby fill the house.

"Hey Dad, turn down that music!" shouted my oldest son, Todd, from the living room. "I'm watching a football game in here." Todd is only eleven but already has a great love for television and is developing quite a knack for lounging around in his pajamas.

In the kitchen my nine-year-old daughter, Gabrielle, or Gabby as we call her, was busy making a leftover turkey sandwich for breakfast when I came in. There were globs of cranberry sauce and mayonnaise splattered on the counter top, plus a trail of sourdough breadcrumbs leading away from the pantry.

This looks familiar, I thought. *Food, Bing, and Football—the Christmas season has officially begun!*

"Okay kids, put on your jackets," I said. "I think it's time we go to the mall. Let's hurry up; I want to beat the holiday rush."

"Why are we going?" asked Gabby as she licked a spot of mustard from her finger.

"Well, so you can tell Santa what you want for Christmas this year."

"But Dad," moaned Todd. "Aren't we too old for that?"

"You're never too old, Son. Besides, I have it on very good authority they have a new Santa Claus at the mall this year—one like you've never seen before. He's expecting you."

"Why would he be expecting us?" asked Todd.

"Well," said Lynn as she joined us in the kitchen. "Let's just say he's an old friend of ours."

❖ ❖ ❖

The trip to the mall was more eventful than expected, but that's another story altogether. Santa gave both children a candy cane and a slip of paper with an address on it. Their first night as elves at the Children's Hospital will be tomorrow, and I can hardly wait. Dr. Amburi is Chief of Staff there now and says he has big plans for this year's Christmas Pageant.

After the mall we came home and began to decorate with lights, wreaths, and every Christmassy thing we own. Lynn found a safe spot in the house for each of her Nativity scenes, then let the children take turns arranging the figurines around the various baby Jesus'. While we were decorating the Christmas tree Todd asked me to tell him again about the white, worn out, old paper bag with holes in it that we place on top of the tree each year.

"Well," I cautioned. "I can't really tell you about the bag without telling you the whole story of my first real Christmas. You sure you're up for that?"

"Yeah," said Todd. "I want to hear it again. It's tradition. Gabby! Come sit down. Dad's going to tell us about his old bag."

"Okay," I began. "It was the day after Thanksgiving, 1980, that marked the beginning of my first Christmas ever. As a nine-year-old boy I had certainly celebrated the revered holiday plenty of times before, but that particular Christmas was the first one that really mattered. It was the type of experience that makes you wish Christmas was celebrated all year long; the kind that makes people forget about life's imperfections and focus instead on it's greatest treasures such as family, friendship, and serving others. For me, it was a defining moment, one that has shaped and molded the very fabric of my soul.

"As with many Christmas stories, mine began on Santa's lap. But this was no ordinary Santa, and he had anything but an ordinary lap."